# LIAR

### Kathy Lee

Each *Seasiders* story is complete in itself – but if you enjoy this book, you may like to read the others in the series:

# Runners

# Joker

# Winner

The same people (plus some new ones!) appear in all the books.

Scripture Union

*The Lord is near to those who call to him.*
    (Psalm 145 verse 18, from the *Good News Bible*)

© Kathy Lee 2000
First Published 2000

Scripture Union, 207–209 Queensway, Bletchley, Milton Keynes
MK2 2EB, England

ISBN 1 85999 357 5

British Library Cataloguing-in-Publication Data.
A catalogue record of this book is available from the British
Library.

Printed and bound in Great Britain by Cox & Wyman Ltd,
Reading.

# Contents

For Gwen, who told me all about garter snakes

# Chapter 1

## Normal

"What's your name?"

It's a perfectly normal question, but it still made me freeze up inside.

"Katie," I would always say, to give myself time to think. And by the time they asked, "Katie who?" I would have remembered what my surname was meant to be. Katie Martin... Katie Wilson... no, Katie Gray...

The name kept changing, see. It was very confusing. For two years I felt as if I didn't know who I was. And now, when it's safe to go back to my real name – Katie Martin, the one I was born with – I still feel sort of mixed up. Who am I really? Where do I belong?

It's quite safe now. He's in prison and there's nothing to be scared of any more. I keep telling myself that. I keep telling Mam, too... but she still has the nightmares.

"Wake up, Mam! Wake up! You've been dreaming again."

It's really hard to wake her sometimes. She gets hold of me so tight that it hurts, and screams, "No! No! You're not taking my Katie!"

"Mam, let go. Mam! It's just a dream. It's not really happening."

And then, like a drowning person struggling up to the surface, she fights her way up out of the dream. She'll be trembling, gasping for breath. She'll look around as if she doesn't have a clue where she is. (Mind you, that's not surprising, we've lived in so many different places.)

And then I get her a drink and we talk for a while. It's best if she doesn't go straight back to sleep, because the dream can take over again.

"I'm sorry, my love," she always says. "Waking you up like that. Never mind. Have a lie-in tomorrow, eh?"

"I can't, Mam. It's school."

"Oh, school. Won't hurt you to miss a day now and then."

She says that because for almost two years I didn't go to school at all. Do you think that sounds good? It wasn't. It was terrible. I got so bored just hanging around while Mam was working. And when she had time off, she would be trying to teach me the things I should have been doing at school.

Worst of all, I had nobody to play with. No friends, except the kids who stayed at whatever hotel we were in – and they were only there for a week or two.

Sometimes, if it was term time, people would wonder why I wasn't at school. And Mam would say, "Oh, we've only just arrived here in Blackpool" (or Scarborough, or wherever). "She'll be starting school next term." But I knew that by next term we would have moved on again. We never stayed anywhere for long.

Mam usually found work as a hotel chambermaid, cleaning rooms and making beds. Not the world's most fascinating job – but at least it gave us a place to live, and free meals (sometimes delicious, sometimes terrible).

Hotel staff are always coming and going. If people asked too many questions about us, Mam would decide it was time to move on somewhere else. You can't be too careful, she was always telling me. Don't do anything that will make people notice you. If *he* gets on our trail again...

But now he was in prison. He would be locked up for years. We were safe, and we could start to live a normal life again... or try to.

We live in a town called Westhaven, at the Sea View Hotel. It isn't much compared with some of the places that we've stayed in, but the people are nice. Mr and Mrs Thorne – Terry and Lisa – run the place. They have two boys. David is ten, the same age as me, and Jake is two years older.

David's all right, I suppose. I mean, he's quite friendly most of the time, except at school. Just because we walked to school together once or twice, people were saying he was my boyfriend. He got all embarrassed and stopped talking to me at school.

But Jake's the one I really like. He saved my life once. He's really brave. He and his friend Neddy rescued me after I was kidnapped. I wouldn't mind people thinking *he* was my boyfriend... but he never seems to notice me much. (Except to get annoyed if I beat him at snooker.)

The Sea View Hotel is in Fountain Square.

"Where's the fountain?" visitors always ask, because there isn't one. What used to be a fountain is just a headless statue covered in seagull droppings. What used to be a pool is an empty circle of stone. The whole area is a bit like that – "gone down in the world", Mam says.

It must have been quite posh a hundred years ago, when each of the tall, thin houses belonged to one family. Nowadays they've been split up into flats, or turned into antique shops. So there are not many kids living in the Square. I vaguely knew Jake's friends, Ben and Neddy. Ben had a sister, Grace, who was my age, but I had hardly ever spoken to her. She spent most of her time with Megan from the Corner Café.

"Why don't you walk to school with those two?" asked Mam. "You know I don't like you going on your own." (This was after David had decided he wasn't going to be seen with me in public.)

"Oh, *Mam*. I'm nearly eleven. I can cross the road on my own, you know."

She still looked anxious. "I'd take you myself if I wasn't working. Why don't you walk with that girl Grace? She seems nice."

"She's got a friend already – they don't want me. Look, Mam, what are you worried about? He's in prison. You don't need to be anxious, not any more."

Mam sighed. "I know, love. But it's a hard habit to break. Go on then, hurry up, or you'll be late for your precious school."

# Chapter 2

## Drama

I didn't mind being a new girl at school. I've never been quiet and shy – I'm not like Mam, hating to be noticed. It was quite fun being the centre of attention.

Some people had read in the papers about how I was kidnapped and rescued a few weeks before. They wanted to know all about it. The trouble was, I couldn't actually remember much; I had been unconscious most of the time.

But that sounded boring, so I found myself talking about what I would have seen, if only I'd been awake. "He threw me in the back of his car and drove away at eighty miles an hour –"

"Didn't you try to get out?" said one of the girls who was listening. "*I* would have."

"Yes, but he'd locked all the doors. I banged on the window, and then he told me to shut up or else he'd kill me. He had a gun, of course." (No he didn't, except in my imagination, but who was to know?)

"Why did he kidnap you? For money?"

"He did it because he hates my Mam. He wanted to get back at her for something that happened long ago."

I told them about how, when she was young, Mam

used to go out with this guy called Paul. But he was already married. He killed his wife and tried to make it look like an accident. Then he got Mam to tell lies to the police.

In the end, though, Mam told the truth when Paul came to trial, and he was sent to prison. Ever after that he hated her and swore he would get his revenge. (All this part was perfectly true, by the way.)

Mam felt safe while he was in prison. She got married and had a baby – me – and lived an ordinary life, although my dad didn't stick around for very long. Then, when I was about eight, Mam got the news that Paul was being released from jail. That was when we went on the run.

"Oh! Was it exciting?" said someone. By now there was quite a crowd of people, all standing round me listening.

"Sometimes it was exciting." To be honest, most of the time it was really boring. But that wasn't what they wanted to hear.

"Tell us. Tell us what happened."

I wanted them to go on listening. I tried to remember something – anything – that would make a good story. But then the bell rang for the end of break. A sigh of disappointment went up.

"I'll tell you tomorrow," I said, feeling relieved. By then I would have managed to think of something, or invent something. (Well, not invent exactly. I would use what really happened and just liven it up a bit... I was good at doing that.)

This kind of thing – having people my own age to talk to – was the good side of school. The actual lessons were the bad side.

Mam had tried to keep me up with my schoolwork during the two years of no school. She had taught me all the things she could remember learning when she was my age. In maths, I knew my tables really well, and I could do complicated sums without a calculator. But other kinds of maths were a total blank. What was a bar chart? What did "symmetrical" mean?

Other lessons were just the same. I was brilliant in some areas and hopeless in others. The teacher, Mrs Duncan, didn't know which group to put me in. The class couldn't decide whether I was a genius or an idiot.

There was one subject I always enjoyed – Drama. (Guess what I want to be when I grow up?) One day Mrs Duncan told us we were going to start rehearsing for the school play, which would be put on at the end of term. "Who would like to have a speaking part?" she asked.

Most of the girls' hands shot up, mine included. The boys were a lot less keen.

"Luckily, in this play, most of the characters are animals," Mrs Duncan said. "So it doesn't matter whether they are boys or girls. But we do need a few boys in speaking parts. I want four volunteers..."

When none of the boys volunteered, she picked the four nearest. David was one of them; he looked panic-stricken.

"Today we're going to read through the play, to get an idea of what it's all about. It's called *The Enchanted Forest*. The part you will read this morning probably won't be the one you end up playing, but I would still like you to do your best. Put some expression in your voice as you read – don't just gabble."

She chose people at random to read the various parts. I was someone called Princess Esmeralda. Flicking through the script, I saw that Esmeralda had quite a lot to say; she was one of the main characters. Maybe, if I read well, I would be chosen to play her.

At least I looked the part of a princess, I thought. My face was pretty enough, and I had long, wavy hair which was mostly blonde. (My natural hair colour is brown – Mam used to dye it when we were in hiding, as a sort of disguise. There was no need for that now, but the blonde bits were still growing out.)

When it was my turn to read, I put on the posh voice that I had learned from listening to rich people in hotels.

"Servants! Bring me my fur-lined robe and my second-best crown. At once, I say! What do you mean by keeping me waiting?"

Some people giggled, but Mrs Duncan stopped them. "That was very good, Katie. You remembered what I said about using expression in your voice. Carry on."

My next bit was less successful. I said a word wrong. It was the word *consider*. "I consider that a very foolish remark." I said the word as if it rhymed with *outsider*. Mrs Duncan corrected me; I felt embarrassed.

A few minutes later it happened again. This time the word *monarch* tripped me up. I said it as if it should rhyme with *march*. Well, how was I to know? I hadn't read aloud to anyone for ages.

It wasn't that I was a bad reader. Reading was one way to pass the time when we were in hiding; I often tried to lose myself in a book. (If there were any around, that is. It's amazing how many hotels seem to think their customers can't read.) But when I came to a word I didn't know, reading alone while Mam was at work, I had nobody to ask about it. I just had to guess, or skip over it and carry on.

How many other words were waiting to trip me up? How many times would Mrs Duncan have to correct me? I began to lose confidence. I started to mumble my words, so that if I did make a mistake nobody would hear.

Mrs Duncan looked as if she was going to say something; then she changed her mind. I struggled through to the end of the play, knowing that I would never get a main part now. I would end up being a tortoise or something, with about two lines to say. Or a tree, with no lines at all.

I felt miserable as I walked home that day. To take my mind off things, I let my thoughts slide off into a day-dream. It was the day of the play, and everyone was panicking, because Princess Esmeralda hadn't arrived. She had been taken ill with food-poisoning.

"What on earth can we do? We can't perform the play without her. Nobody else knows her lines."

Then (in the day-dream) I stepped forward. "I do. I know all the lines." And I proved it by reciting them, word-perfect.

Everyone looked at me doubtfully. "You really think you can do it, Katie?" asked the teacher.

"Of course."

And I amazed them all with my performance. I was much better than the girl who'd been chosen for the part. At the end everyone clapped and cheered and shouted my name...

"Oi! Katie!"

I stopped. That wasn't part of the day-dream.

Someone had really called my name.

Looking round, I saw Megan and Grace coming up behind me. So far, I didn't much like what I'd seen of Megan. At school she was always trying to get other people into trouble. She had dark hair cut in a spiky fringe above her sharp, mean little eyes.

She said, "Oh look, it's Princess Esmeralda. The reigning mon-*arch*."

I tried to smile to show I didn't care. It was difficult.

"You think you're oh so wonderful," said Megan. "You think you're better than everybody else. And you can't even read!"

"Stop it, Megan," said Grace. She was small, with fair curly hair and a face that smiled easily. She looked like the Good Fairy in a pantomime. (And Megan was the Bad Fairy. Why were they friends?)

Megan glared at me. "You show off all the time. You make me sick. Well, they won't choose you as the Princess now, will they? Ha ha!"

Now I was angry. "I suppose you think you might get chosen," I said.

"Yeah. Why not? At least I can read words of more than three letters."

"I'll tell you why not. Because the princess is supposed to be beautiful. Before *you* could be the princess, you'd need plastic surgery."

Her fists clenched. "You calling me ugly?"

"I wouldn't be so rude. I do think you should try for the part of the Hippopotamus, though. You'd be ideal for it."

"Oh stop it, both of you," said Grace, but we hardly heard her.

"You call me ugly one more time," Megan hissed,

"and I'll smash your face in."

"Ugly one more time," I said, grinning at her.

She took a wild swing at me. I moved aside, and she hit her knuckles on the wall behind me. Now she looked absolutely furious. Maybe *I* would be the one needing plastic surgery, if things got out of hand.

"What's this? Fighting in a public highway?" said a voice I knew.

It was Jake. He was on his way home from school with his friend Ben, and another boy – Megan's big brother Darren.

"Can't you keep your sister under control, Darren?" said Jake.

"Nah," said Darren. "Mum and Dad can't, so how do you expect me to? Go on, get off home," he said to Megan. "Else I'll tell Dad you were fighting again."

"Wasn't fighting," said Megan sulkily. "*She* called me ugly."

"So? You are ugly," said her kind brother. "Go on home. You make the street look messy."

"I hate you," Megan muttered to me. "You wait. I'm going to get you."

Ben said, "Mummy mummy, I hate Johnny's guts... Well leave them on the side of the plate, then." I think he was trying to be funny, but no one laughed.

I went back to Sea View with the boys. Well, not exactly *with* them, since they hardly noticed me. They were talking about boring old football. But I felt safer walking along beside them. Megan wouldn't dare to try anything when Jake was around. Jake had come to my rescue again.

Oh, if only he liked me... if only he didn't think I was just a kid...

# Chapter 3

## Old memories

In the old days Mam hardly ever went out anywhere. She said it was safer not to. She was always worried that Paul would somehow manage to track us down.

Now she was gradually getting less timid. On her afternoons off we usually went out, even if it was only for a walk. (We didn't have the money for places like the theatre or the fun fair, except as a special treat. But walking cost nothing at all.)

We explored Westhaven – the old part by the harbour, the New Town (which is actually two hundred years old) and the modern shopping mall. Mam still didn't like crowded places much. She would look around nervously, and keep a tight hold of my hand.

Often I felt impatient with her. I wished she was more like other people's mums, who chatted and smiled and yelled at their kids without a care in the world. And I wished I had a dad like other people's dads. Someone strong, loving and gentle. Someone who would take care of us...

Now and then I asked her about my dad. I didn't remember him at all; he had gone away when I was just a baby. Mam didn't even have a photo of him. Did he really exist?

"Oh, he existed all right." Mam's voice sounded bitter. "Still does, for all I know. Or care."

Usually she would refuse to say more. Her mouth would close in a grim, tight line. If I went on asking questions, she would get angry. "He was a no-good, useless so-and-so, and I don't want to talk about him." Then she would be in a bad mood for ages.

But sometimes, if she'd had a drink or two, she would talk about the past. About how she met my dad – they were both working in the same hotel – and how good-looking he was. "You've got his big brown eyes, Katie. And his smile. I remember him holding you, smiling down at you..."

"He didn't hate me, then?"

"Hate you? No. What makes you think that?"

I said awkwardly, "I thought maybe he went away because he didn't like me. Didn't like having a baby around."

"Oh no. He was fond enough of you."

"Why did he leave, then?"

Her face darkened. "He left because he met somebody else. He'd been seeing her for ages. Lying to me, saying he was working late, when he was going out with her. Then when I found out, I said he had to choose – her or me."

"And he chose her."

"Yes. So I said to him, right, don't ever expect to see Katie, ever again. I took you to live with my mum – your Nan. He came round once or twice, wanting to see you, but I never let him. Last I heard he'd gone away to London."

I wondered where he was now. Did he ever think of

me, the baby he'd smiled at as he held me in his arms? I thought of him often. When I was old enough, I meant to go to London and look for him. Or get on one of those TV shows where they find your long-lost relatives.

Of course I never mentioned this to Mam. She would only get angry. She'd start telling me how bad he was, a cheat and a liar, not to be trusted. She would say we didn't need him. "Haven't I looked after you all these years, without a penny from him? We don't want anything to do with him. Forget him, Katie."

One day when we were out walking, Mam stopped outside a second-hand shop. There are quite a few of them in Westhaven. Some are proper antique shops, with one beautiful, polished table in the window, and snooty assistants who stare at you. Others are just heaps of junk.

This place was somewhere in between. The shop window was crammed with hundreds of things – ornaments, vases, silver fish-knives, necklaces, teapots, clocks. They were all old, if not antique.

"Oh Katie, look!" said Mam, pointing at one of the crowded shelves. "Your Nan used to have one just like that."

"What? You mean the potty?"

"No, no. The china flower girl. There. Don't you remember? It used to sit on her mantelpiece. If you were very good she used to take it down and let you look at it."

"Oh... yes, I do remember." All at once, like a flashback in a film, I could picture Nan's cosy sitting-room, with the cat curled up on a sofa, the chiming clock, the tin of toffees, the little velvet chair that was just for me. That was the house we lived in until I was six, when Nan died.

"I wonder how much they're asking for that," said Mam. We went into the shop. She asked if we could have a closer look at the china lady.

It was exactly like Nan's one. I remembered the details – each flower in the basket perfectly shaped, each fold of the dress... The flower girl smiled at me as she used to long ago, when I was small and carefree and happy.

"Is it the same one?" I asked.

Mam laughed. "I expect there are hundreds of these around. Your Nan dropped hers one day when she was dusting, and it smashed on the tiles. She was upset, all right. Don't you remember?"

No, I couldn't remember that. But other memories were starting to come back. The books Nan read to me, the smell of baking, the budgie chirping in his cage...

"Mam, I wish we could buy this," I said. "It's so nice to remember Nan's house."

I saw the same longing in her own face. "How much is it?" she asked.

"Thirty-five pounds," the shop lady said, and Mam hastily put the flower girl down. She turned to go.

"I *could* let you have it for thirty," said the woman.

"No, sorry. We can't afford it," said Mam. "Thank you for letting us look, though. Brought back old times."

She pulled me out of the shop. "Now don't start," she said, before I'd opened my mouth. "We can't afford it and that's that. Thirty quid for a bit of china! And it would only get broken."

I said nothing. It would be Mam's birthday in a couple of months, and now I knew the ideal present.

Thirty quid, though. Where on earth would I find that kind of money? Thirty quid might as well be thirty thousand, or thirty million...

Day-dreaming, I planned what to do if I won the Lottery. Everyone crowded round, wondering what I would spend the money on. Reporters jostled with TV cameramen. "What are you going to buy first, Katie?"

And I would surprise them all. Not a house, a car or a trip to Disneyworld – but a china flower girl for Mam.

# Chapter 4

## Henry

Jake's mum, Lisa, is really nice. You can see where Jake gets his good looks from, his fair hair and lively blue eyes. Because of the hotel, Lisa is always busy, and yet she never makes you feel as if you're wasting her time. She was the only person I told about my need for money; I knew she would help if she could.

"Well, now. How would you like to do a few jobs around the place?" she said. "You could earn some extra pocket-money that way. You're a good little worker – much better than David and Jake."

For the rest of the week I helped her clear tables in the dining-room. I didn't mind that. What I didn't like was stacking the dirty plates in the dishwasher – because that meant entering the kitchen. And the kitchen was Henry's kingdom.

For some reason, Henry took against Mam and me right from the start. He was always grumbling about us, trying to stir up trouble. Lisa told us to take no notice – it was only because we were new, and Henry disliked change of any sort. But all the same it wasn't very nice.

I noticed that Jake and David often got better food

than Mam and me. If they didn't like what was on the menu that day, Henry would cook them something they did like. Mam and I had to take what we were given.

"You ought to be grateful," Henry would mutter. "I don't see why I should be feeding two people when only one of them earns it." He meant that for Mam, three meals a day was part of her wages, but I was an extra. A hanger-on, a nuisance.

"This food doesn't belong to you," I pointed out to him. "You didn't pay for it, you only cooked it. Why should you care?"

Henry snorted. "Only cooked it? *Only* cooked it? If you don't believe that matters, young miss, then you can have your meat raw tomorrow, with the blood still oozing out."

"Fine," I said. "I was thinking of going vegetarian anyway." I helped myself to a chocolate eclair, and was off before he could stop me. (He's so big and fat, there's no way he could catch me up.)

Mam told me off later for being cheeky. "It's downright stupid," she said. "If you must go making enemies for yourself, pick on somebody else. Not the people we've got to live with and work with."

"Henry would still hate us whatever we do," I said.

"Maybe, but that doesn't mean you can be rude to him. I thought you liked it here at Sea View."

"I do like it," I said.

"Well behave yourself, then. I don't want trouble. If there's trouble, then we're off."

"What do you mean?" I asked, alarmed.

"We did it before, we can do it again. We'll move on somewhere else. Some other town. Start all over again."

"No! No, Mam. I don't want that. I want to stay here – I'll be good. Honest."

So I was extra careful whenever I went into the kitchen. Most of the time, though, Henry simply ignored me. He walked past me as if I wasn't there. I kept feeling the urge to stick my foot out and trip him up. (Henry falling over would be a majestic and awesome sight, like the *Titanic* going down.)

But I was good. I behaved myself. At the end of the week, Lisa said what a help I'd been, and gave me five pounds. I was very grateful, although at this rate it would take me six weeks to save thirty pounds. What if someone else bought the flower seller first?

Lisa said, "Why don't you ask if you can put down a deposit on it?"

"A what?"

"A deposit. Some shops let people do that. Pay what you can afford, and they promise to keep the thing for you until you can save the rest of the money."

It was worth a try. On Saturday morning, while Mam was working, I took my five pounds down to the shop. A different woman was in charge today. She was middle-aged and smartly dressed, with the sort of hairstyle that stays in place even in a Force Ten gale. She wore more rings, brooches and necklaces than I'd ever seen on one person.

"Yes, of course you can put down a deposit, dear," she said. "Five pounds? That will be thirty still to pay."

"Oh," I said, taken aback. "The other lady said we could have it cheaper. Thirty pounds altogether, she said."

The woman looked doubtful. "When was this?"

"Only last weekend." I gave her a pleading look.

"It's for a present for my Mam. I haven't got much money. It's going to take me weeks to save up..."

"Oh, very well then. Thirty," she said, although I could tell she didn't want to.

I had a sudden idea. "Er... I don't suppose you need any help around here? I'm really good at dusting and polishing and that. Whatever I earn, you could put towards paying for the flower girl."

She looked horrified. "No, dear. I couldn't possibly risk it. Lots of these things are valuable, you know."

My face must have shown my disappointment. But just as I was going, she said, "Wait a minute. There is a way you might be able to help me."

"Yes?"

"Next Sunday I'm off on a buying trip. I'll go round the villages, knocking on doors, to see if anyone has things they want to sell. That's where most of my stock comes from." She waved an arm at the things on display.

"Okay," I said. "What do you want me to do – look after the shop?"

"No, no. I want you to come with me."

"But why? I don't know the first thing about antiques."

"You don't need to know anything, dear. All you have to do is look at people with those big brown eyes of yours, that can charm the birds out of the trees. Old ladies adore pretty little girls. If you do the talking, I'll do the buying."

It sounded a bit odd to me. But it would be more fun than dusting or clearing tables.

"How much would I get paid?"

"That depends. Five pounds, maybe ten if we have

a good day."

Ten pounds! "I'll do it," I said at once. In my excitement I forgot all Mam's warnings about not trusting a stranger.

"Good girl. But you must make sure it's all right with your mum, won't you?"

"Yes, of course I will," I said untruthfully. I wanted Mam's present to be a surprise. She mustn't find out what I was doing. I would tell her Grace or somebody had asked me out for the day.

I almost danced out of the shop. Charm the birds out of the trees... I began to plan what I would wear next Sunday. Not jeans and trainers. Old ladies probably preferred something a bit old-fashioned, like that flowery dress I hardly ever wore. And a hair-band – I would look just like Alice in Wonderland.

I stopped suddenly. Ahead of me a big, stout figure was ambling along. It looked like Henry; this must be his day off. What did Henry do, I wondered, on his day off? Go out for a posh meal that someone else had cooked? Go to McDonalds?

What he did surprised me. He crossed the street towards a building called the Reptile House. It was one of Westhaven's tourist attractions – somewhere for visitors to go when it was too cold or wet for the beach.

Mam and I had visited it once. We both agreed it was a waste of money. None of the snakes seemed to do very much, just lay there in their glass-fronted cages, as bored as the people viewing them. The two small alligators looked and behaved exactly like logs of wood. The tortoise could have been a plastic model – it was hard to tell.

Was Henry interested in reptiles, then? He was

definitely going in there. I must tell Jake – I was sure he didn't know about this. No one at Sea View had ever mentioned snakes in connection with Henry.

I imagined a cobra or rattlesnake escaping from its cage, slithering up behind Henry, and sinking its fangs in his big fat leg. An ambulance screeched to a halt. Henry was carted off to hospital, never again to appear at Sea View... Well, I could dream, couldn't I?

# Chapter 5

## Film star

On Monday I saw Grace walking to school by herself. I hurried to catch her up.

"No Megan today, then?" I said, trying not to sound pleased about it.

"She's off sick. She's got that tummy bug that's going round."

"Tummy bug? Could be nasty. I wonder if all their customers will get it too."

Megan's mum and dad ran a café on the corner of Fountain Square. It was a bit of a dump. When you went past, you got blasted with loud music and the smell of greasy chips. Older kids sat in there all day, or stood on the pavement outside, drinking cans of lager. Mam had told me to avoid the place.

"Why?"

"I don't like the crowd that hangs around there. They look like trouble."

Trouble – that was certainly true of Megan. I said to Grace, "How come you and Megan are friends? I mean, do you actually like her?"

"Yes... at least I used to. She used to be okay. We've always been friends, ever since nursery."

"Used to be okay? You mean she wasn't born stirring up trouble and picking fights?"

Grace said, "She was all right before her mum left."

I didn't understand. "I thought that was her mum working in the café."

"Oh, she's come back again. She went away for months, and Megan's dad was talking about getting divorced. That's when Megan started playing up. Everybody noticed it, even the teachers. Then her mum came back, and I hoped Megan would go back to normal, but she didn't. I think she's scared her mum will do it again."

"Why did she leave?"

"They were always having rows, her mum and dad. They still fight, even though they're supposed to be together again. I've heard them sometimes. It's really horrible."

I thought to myself that Megan had nothing much to grumble about. Even a father who shouted all the time was better than no father at all.

Grace said, "*My* mum and dad never shout at each other. They hardly even argue. Do yours?"

"Mine haven't had an argument in ten whole years. Possibly because they haven't seen each other in ten whole years."

"Oh. Are they divorced?"

"Yeah – my dad walked out when I was a baby. I don't even know what he looked like."

For some reason Grace was easy to talk to. I found myself telling her things that I'd never told anybody else. How I missed my dad, even though I couldn't remember him... how I day-dreamed that he was rich and famous, a film star or something... how I longed to meet him one day. She listened, looking thoughtful.

"But I don't know how I'm ever going to find him," I said gloomily. "He went off to London years ago. God only knows where he is now. He could be in Australia."

"Or he could be walking down this very street," said Grace.

"Yes, and I wouldn't recognise him. It's hopeless."

Grace said, "My mum says nothing's ever hopeless – not if you pray about it."

I looked at her blankly. She said, "*God only knows where he is now*. That's what you said, and it's true. God does know."

"Fine, except I don't happen to believe in God."

"I do. I'll pray about it if you like."

"What, now? Right here in the street?" I said, surprised. I thought she would have to kneel down and close her eyes.

Instead, she walked on in silence for a minute as if she was thinking. Then she turned to me and grinned.

"Did you do it?" I said. "What did you ask for exactly?"

"For you to find your real father."

It was a prayer that would be answered – but not in the way I expected.

At school I wasn't the New Girl any more. There was somebody else even newer – a boy called Elliot, from California. He was a real show-off, always talking about Disneyland and Hollywood and "when I lived in L.A."

One day, when he was boasting yet again about

some film star he'd seen at a pizza parlour, I got really annoyed.

"So what if he's met a few film stars?" I said loudly. "My dad *is* a film star."

Several heads turned towards me.

"Is he? You never said."

"What's his name?"

"If your dad's a film star, how come you don't live in Hollywood?"

I said, "My Mam met him before he was famous. They got divorced because he went off with somebody else. He went to America and she never heard from him for years. Until one day she saw his name on a film poster..."

"Who is this guy?" said Elliot, looking as if he didn't believe a word.

"I'm not allowed to say. It's a secret."

Megan said, "Strange. I can't think of a single film star with the surname Martin."

"Oh, he has a stage name, of course," I said airily.

"But why do you have to keep it a secret?" someone asked.

"Because he's got married again and has kids. He's got this image, see – the perfect father, the all-American family. He doesn't want anyone to know about Mam and me. Of course he sends us some money now and then..."

"I don't believe you," Megan said. "You're making it up."

"Believe what you like," I said carelessly. "But don't be surprised if you go to the cinema and see someone who reminds you of me. Same eyes, same smile."

After that I shut up and refused to say any more – which is the best way of making people curious. I could see that quite a few of them believed everything I'd said.

Not Grace, though. She knew the truth all right – and she gave me a funny look.

I just hoped she would manage not to tell Megan.

# Chapter 6

## Your father's daughter

We had started rehearsing for the play. Another girl, Charlotte, had been chosen as the Princess. I didn't mind too much – at least Megan didn't get the part.

I was to be a squirrel (don't laugh – the squirrel was actually quite a good part with a fair amount to say). Megan, much to my delight, was a snake. Typecast or what? David was chosen as the dashing Prince Edmund, who married the Princess in the end.

"Oh no," he muttered. "That means I have to kiss Charlotte. Yuk! I don't even want to be in the stupid play. How can I get out of it?"

"You could always pretend to be ill," I suggested.

"What, from now until June? They wouldn't believe me."

"Fall downstairs and break a leg, then. You couldn't act the handsome Prince Edmund with your leg in plaster." I was joking, but David looked almost desperate enough to try it.

When Jake heard about the play, he started taking the mickey out of David. (Jake and David are so nasty to each other it makes me glad I'm an only child.) He called David "Prince Head-wound" or "Prince

Ethelbert" or "The Clown Prince of Moronia". If he answered the phone to a friend of David's, he would say, "I'm dreadfully sorry, his royal highness is at present unavailable, as he is in the toilet."

I needed someone to help me learn my lines. It was no good asking David – *he* wouldn't know if I was pronouncing things properly. Would Jake help me?

I chose the wrong moment to ask. He'd just got hold of a new computer game, and he was playing it non-stop. "Get lost, Katie," he said. "I'm busy. Why don't you ask your mum?"

Mam said, "Is this what they're teaching you at school? Waste of time, if you ask me. You ought to be learning something useful."

"It *is* useful," I said. "It's all good practice for when I grow up. I think I'll be an actress when I grow up, Mam."

"You will not," Mam said. "That's one thing you are not going to be. You'll do a good, honest job where you can earn a decent living. Acting!" She snorted.

"But acting is a good job, Mam. Lots of actors get to be rich and famous."

"Yes, some do. The lucky ones. But there are thousands more that never get rich and famous. They struggle on doing dead-end jobs, waiting for their big chance, but it never comes. You may be your father's daughter, but I'm not having you wasting your life like that."

Your father's daughter... "What do you mean?" I asked. "Was my dad an actor, then? I thought you said he worked in a hotel."

"He did. He worked as a waiter because he couldn't get enough acting jobs to make a living. Resting, he called it. He was always telling me things would change – I believed him at first. But he was just kidding himself."

"Wasn't he any good, then?"

"Oh, he was good. But there were lots of other people that were even better." She put her arm round me. "Don't let me depress you, love. You enjoy your play-acting if you want to. Just forget all that rich and famous stuff, okay?"

Depress me? She hadn't depressed me at all. I knew now that one bit of my day-dream – my father the actor – was absolutely true. Maybe the rest of it would come true one day, too...

On Sunday, I was to be at the antique shop for half past ten. I told Mam I was going to Grace's for lunch; she looked pleased. Just in case she was watching from the window, I went across the Square and knocked at Grace's house. I meant to ask if I could go in at the front door and out at the back.

Nobody answered my knock. I tried again.

"What are you doing here?" said a hostile voice from behind me. It was Megan.

"Grace asked me over," I said. "What's it to you?"

"You're such a liar," she said. "Grace is *my* friend, not yours. She never asked you over."

"Yes she did. You don't own her, do you?"

"Liar. She's not even there, they've all gone to church."

She could be right; no one seemed to be in. Quickly I walked away from the house, hoping Mam hadn't seen me. Although Mam had spent two years telling fibs to everyone we met, she absolutely hated being lied to. Especially by me.

Megan followed me. "Where are you going?" she asked nosily.

"The ice rink." It was the first place that popped into my mind.

"Oh sure," she said, "you look as if you're dressed for skating. Why do you have to tell lies all the time?"

"I don't. I never lie," I said, grinning at her. "I have never told a single lie in my entire life."

She chanted, "Liar, liar, pants on fire, halfway up a telephone wire."

"Well, I must go," I said. "Nice talking to you. Oops... I lied."


"Call me Aunt Elaine," said the lady from the antique shop.

Somehow, I couldn't. She was not an aunty sort of person; there was something about her that made me feel nervous. In my mind I called her by her surname, Mrs Parkes, and when I spoke to her I didn't call her anything at all.

We were driving out of town in her car, which was an estate car with lots of room in the boot. "I sometimes buy pieces of furniture, so I need a big car. But mostly I deal in smaller items. You know the kind of thing – you've seen it in the shop."

"Where are we going?" I asked.

"A couple of villages on the far side of Gullford."

"Gullford? But that's miles away. Why not somewhere a bit nearer?"

She laughed. "I've already covered most of the local villages. It doesn't do to go back to the same places too often."

"Why not?"

"People get suspicious. Not that there's anything illegal about what I do," she said hastily. "But I have to make a bit of a profit, or else I'd go out of business."

That meant, I supposed, buying things as cheaply as she could and selling them as dear as she could. I wondered how much my china lady had cost her. Perhaps she had only paid a couple of quid for it.

As if reading my thoughts, she said, "I do provide a useful service, you know. If I didn't buy these things, they would sit collecting dust at the back of a cupboard, and perhaps get thrown away when the owner died. People don't realise the value of things."

We drove on in silence. I could tell we were going inland, but I hadn't much idea where we were. I'd never been in this part of the country. There were wooded hills, steep valleys, and the kind of cute little villages that you see on jigsaw boxes.

I began to feel a bit nervous. Wasn't I doing what Mam had always warned me against – going off in a stranger's car? Not a total stranger, but near enough. I knew her name and where she worked, but apart from that I knew nothing about her.

And I had been so careful to keep things secret. If I went missing, no one would have the slightest clue where I was...

# Chapter 7

## Antiques

As we drove on and on, I made plans in my head and rejected them one by one. Open the door and jump out. Wait till we stop, *then* open the door and jump out. Shout for help if we pass a police station. Write a note and slip it out of the window...

It was just as well I didn't put any of these plans into action. When at last we stopped, in another jigsaw-box village, I saw that my imagination had been overheating again. We were going to do exactly what Mrs Parkes had said – buy antiques.

She didn't bother to try every house. She told me, "My best customers are elderly. They've got things stored up from long ago. Younger people don't often have anything worth looking at."

So we avoided the houses with toys in the garden or jeans on the washing line. That still left plenty of other places to try. Sometimes there was no one in. Sometimes people said, "Sorry, no, we don't buy and sell at the door." One or two, though, had things they were prepared to sell.

"I have some rings I never wear," said one old lady. "Would you like to look at them? Just wait here, if you wouldn't mind. My son tells me never to let strangers come inside, or I'd invite you in." She smiled at me. "But I don't think *you* look the criminal type, my dear."

She went off very slowly into the depths of the house. Mrs Parkes whispered, "When she comes back, ask if you can have a drink of water."

"Why?"

"She might let us in then. I've a feeling this house could be quite interesting. Now don't forget to smile and say please."

I asked for a drink in my most polite, most charming voice.

"Yes, my dear, of course you may. Step inside. I won't be a moment."

It was as easy as that. While she went off to the kitchen, Mrs Parkes looked rapidly into the rooms that opened off the hallway.

For a minute I felt worried again. TV crime programmes often showed old people being robbed by strangers they'd allowed into their homes. Was Mrs Parkes going to steal from the kind old lady? I kept a close eye on her.

But no, she didn't try to steal anything. She simply chatted to the old lady about her collection of china. By the time I'd finished my drink, they had agreed a price for several pieces. Both of them looked happy.

"Well done, Katie," she said as we went back to the car. "I would never have got in there without you."

The same thing happened in two other houses. I began to feel that if I drank one more glass of water, I would explode.

"I think we've finished here," she said at last. "Fancy a spot of lunch?"

We drove out into the country to picnic by the road-side. We had sandwiches, cakes, and a bottle of Coke – although for some reason I wasn't very thirsty. And Mrs Parkes didn't seem to be hungry. She was too busy admiring the things she'd bought.

"This is the best day I've had for ages," she said. "And it's all thanks to you, Katie. Shall we go on to the next village?"

Oh, do we have to? I wanted to say. But I thought of the ten pounds, and tried to look enthusiastic.

She said, "You're *so* good at this – you're an absolute natural. I used to take my niece out with me, before she grew up into a horrible teenager. But she wasn't nearly as appealing as you are."

Of course this made me feel keen to try again. However, in the next village people were less friendly. Only one person let us in, and she didn't have anything worth buying. Mrs Parkes sighed.

"One more for luck, and then we'll go home," she said.

The next house we came to was large and old, with a gravel drive, and stone lions guarding the front door. An old, old man answered our knock. He peered at us short-sightedly. Suddenly his face brightened into a smile.

"Joan! What a lovely surprise! Come in, come in, dear. And this must be little Alice. Haven't you grown?"

I expected Mrs Parkes to explain that we weren't the people he thought we were. But she said nothing, just smiled and motioned at me to go in.

"Sit down. Let me put the kettle on, and then you can tell me all your news." He patted my head. "It's a long time since you came to see your old grandfather, Alice. I've missed you, you know."

I glanced at Mrs Parkes. She put her finger to her lips.

The old man went off to make the tea. Mrs Parkes looked all around the room we sat in; I thought her eyes were greedy. To me, everything in the room seemed antique, even the TV set. But the thing she looked at most was a picture on the wall. Big and old, with a curly gold frame, it showed two horses in a field by a river. It looked rather dark and gloomy, I thought – but she seemed to like it.

The old man poured us each a cup of tea. It was rather a pale colour, almost white. When I sipped it (just to be polite, for I was totally unthirsty), I found out why. He'd forgotten to put any tea in the pot.

He asked how I was getting on at school; I answered somehow. Then he started talking to Mrs Parkes, and I could tell she was fudging her answers, just as I had. But the old man didn't notice. He kept telling us how bad his memory was getting. He could hardly remember which day of the week it was... today, now, must be Wednesday, surely?

"It's Sunday," I said.

"Oh dear me. You see what I mean? I wish I could offer you some buns with your tea, but I forgot to ask whats-her-name to get me any. Never mind."

He talked on and on to Mrs Parkes about people she'd never heard of, whose names he'd forgotten. Getting bored, I picked up a photo album from the coffee-table. It seemed quite old; the photos were small and grey and faded, like looking through the wrong end of a telescope into a time long ago. There was a girl who actually looked a bit like me, playing on the lawn or sitting on a beach.

Then there were no more photos, just blank pages. An ancient yellow newspaper cutting slid out from between them.

"MOTHER AND DAUGHTER KILLED IN CAR CRASH" was the headline. The article told how Joan Taylor (aged 31) and her seven-year-old daughter Alice had died in a road accident. "*Joan Taylor, born Anderson, was the only child of Mr and Mrs Frank Anderson of Ashenbury...*"

That's who he thought we were – his daughter and grandchild, who had been dead for years. He had forgotten their death, along with so much else.

I was so shocked by the discovery, I wanted to run out of the room. Pretending to be someone else, that was one thing. Pretending to be a dead person – that was quite another.

Mrs Parkes was still talking. Somehow she had worked the conversation around to the picture on the wall.

The old man said, "Oh take it – do take it, Joan dear. I can hardly see the thing anyway, my eyes are getting so bad. You may as well have it now as when I'm dead and gone."

"Thank you, Daddy. You *are* kind."

Daddy! It sounded so false, I was sure he would notice. In fact I really hoped he would. But he just sat there, smiling gently.

With that greedy look on her face again, she lifted the horse picture down from its hook. I noticed how carefully she handled it. It must be worth a lot of money.

"And now we must be going. Come along, Kat – er, Alice. Say goodbye to Grandfather."

I said goodbye.

"Come and see me again soon," he said. "Don't leave it so long next time."

"We won't, I promise," she said, kissing him on his wrinkled cheek.

In the car, she didn't notice how quiet I was. She was humming as she drove along.

"How much will you sell the picture for in your shop?" I asked at last.

"Oh, I don't really sell pictures. I haven't the space to display them. But I know a dealer in Brighton who'll give me a good price for it."

I said cautiously, "Wasn't it a bit mean, taking it off the old man?"

"He said himself it was no good to him. He could hardly see it. We didn't *take* it, Katie – he gave it freely. And in return we gave him a nice afternoon which he'll remember for... well, for a little while, until his memory lets him down again."

But I still thought she shouldn't have done it. Especially when she said, "There's no need to mention it to anyone else, though, Katie. It's our little secret, all right?"

Back at the shop, I helped her unload all the things she'd bought. "Have I earned the ten pounds?" I asked her.

"You certainly have. In fact..." She glanced at the flower lady; for a moment I thought she would give it to me there and then. But she changed her mind.

"Come out with me again in a couple of weeks," she said. "Another day like today would be nice, wouldn't it?"

"Yes," I said – lying again. I didn't think it would be nice; actually the whole idea filled me with dread. What had happened that day had left a bad taste in my mouth, worse than the old man's cup of tea.

# Chapter 8

## Bad dreams

In the next few days it wasn't Mam who had nightmares, it was me. I kept dreaming about Alice. She was like a small, faded, black-and-white photo which was alive and moving. We were playing together on the lawn and on the beach. Then her mother called us to get into the car, and I shouted "No!"

But no one listened. No one believed my warnings. We drove along the road towards her grandfather's house, but we never reached it. A huge lorry thundered towards us, out of control. I screamed helplessly as it crashed and crushed us...

Had the little girl come to haunt me because I'd helped to cheat her grandfather? Maybe I would be killed in a car crash, just like her. I had pretended to be Alice, so it was only fair if I died the same way as she did.

I began to feel quite scared. Up till then I'd never thought much about death. It was something that happened to grown-ups; I would worry about it when I got older.

But now I kept thinking of little Alice. She had died

at the age of just seven. She didn't exist any more, except as a pale grey face in a photo. Only her grandfather remembered her, and he would soon be dead too.

That could happen to me. It could happen any time. An illness, a drunk driver, a lorry whose brakes failed, a careless footstep on the stairs... and there would be no more Katie. Wiped out, gone for ever.

I didn't want to die – I really didn't. It would be safer not to take any risks. Don't go roller-blading or swimming. Don't eat meat. Take extra care when crossing the road.

On the way home from school, Victoria Road was busier than usual. I stood on the kerb for ages, waiting for a good long gap in the traffic. Just then Grace came along by herself (Megan was off sick for the third time in a month).

"Are you waiting for a bus?" asked Grace. "They don't stop here, you know."

Embarrassed, I mumbled, "Just trying to cross the road. Mam's always on at me to be careful."

"Oh come on, there's nothing for miles. It's perfectly safe." She grabbed my arm and walked me across the road like a very old lady. "Hey, are you okay? You seem kind of nervous these days. I saw in PE how you didn't want to slide down the rope."

"No. I got scared all of a sudden," I admitted.

"What's the matter?"

I found myself telling her all about my dreams. Of course I didn't mention Mrs Parkes or the painting – just the photo album, the newspaper cutting and the lonely old man. "He was all mixed up, he thought I was his grand-daughter. And now... I know it's really stupid, but I keep worrying... Wouldn't *you* feel a bit weird if it happened to you?"

"Not really. At least I don't think so."

"Aren't you scared of dying, then?"

She shook her head. "Everybody who trusts in God, when they die they go to Heaven."

"Heaven!" I said scornfully. "It doesn't exist. It's just a story they tell to kids when somebody dies." When my Nan died, Mam said she'd gone to Heaven. I was only six, but I could tell Mam didn't really believe what she was saying. Heaven, along with angels and harps and clouds, was a pretend-place – all imagination.

"You're wrong," said Grace. "Heaven's a real place. It's in the Bible." Then she talked about what the Bible said about Heaven – a beautiful city, shining like a jewel, with gates of pearl and streets of gold. The gates would always be open, yet nothing bad would ever be allowed to come in – no sickness or death or pain, no hatred, no lies... She stopped suddenly.

"Pity," I said. "They won't let *me* in, will they?"

I saw by her face that she didn't know what to say.

I said, "Okay, I admit it. I do tell lies sometimes – almost everybody does. So there won't be many people in that beautiful city, will there? Hardly any, I should think. You'll be a bit lonely there, Grace."

"You don't understand," she said. "I'm not saying... I mean, if only the perfectly good people go to Heaven, then it *will* be empty. I won't be allowed in either. But it's not like that."

"What is it like, then?"

She said, "You can still go to Heaven, even if you didn't live a perfect life. Anybody can, as long as they trust in God and are sorry for what they did wrong..."

"I don't understand." How could I trust in a God I didn't believe existed?

"I wish I could explain it better," she said. "My mum would be able to tell you. Come round sometime and we'll ask her."

"Okay. Not today, though. Mam's taking me to get my hair cut," I said, feeling glad of the excuse. Some of the things Grace said made me want to know more. But other bits made me want to cover my ears and pretend I hadn't heard.

What was so very wrong about lying? Like I'd said, everyone did it, even grown-ups. Mam had told lies to save us from our enemy; Mrs Parkes did it for the sake of a painting; Jake's dad did it too, although I wasn't sure why. (I had my suspicions, though.)

Not long before, I'd seen Jake's dad talking on the office phone, only to put it down quickly when he heard Lisa in the hallway.

"Who was that, Terry?" she called to him.

"Oh, nothing. Wrong number."

Which was a lie. You don't smile and laugh when you're talking to a wrong number. You don't look all secretive as you put the phone down. Why was Jake's dad telling lies to his wife?

I told myself to forget it. After all, it was none of my business.

# Chapter 9

## Secrets

I didn't much like my new haircut. It was a lot shorter, cut in layers, and all the blonde bits had gone. My hair was back to its natural colour – dark brown, like my eyes.

A stranger's face looked at me from the mirror. I frowned at her. She frowned back.

"Don't you like it?" asked Mam.

"No, I don't. I look so different!"

She laughed. "You look like you always used to, up until a couple of years ago. It suits you like this, love, it really does."

I was not convinced. "Can't I grow it long again?"

"I suppose so, if you really want to. But you know how tangled it used to get. It's much easier to brush and comb when it's short."

"If that's what you're worried about," I muttered, "why didn't you get my head shaved completely? I wouldn't need a comb at all then." Mam told me not to be so silly.

I wondered what Jake would think of my new hairstyle. If he didn't like it then I would definitely go back to being blonde, even if I had to buy the hair colour and dye it myself.

Jake was in the hotel games room, watching TV. I sat down at the far end of the sofa and said hello. He grunted something. Even when I made some comments about the film he was watching, he hardly looked at me.

Then David came in. "Seen Katie? Oh!" He stopped and stared at me. "Hey Katie, I didn't recognise you. You look really different."

"Yeah, I know. But is it good-different or bad-different?"

"Good... I think. It will take a bit of getting used to, though."

"What do you think, Jake?" I asked. When he didn't answer, I kicked him on the ankle. "My hair. Do you like it or not?"

He glanced at me for about 0.0001 seconds. "S'all right, I suppose. Look, can't you kids go somewhere else if you want to talk? I'm trying to watch the telly."

I got annoyed then. I decided he was going to notice me whether he wanted to or not.

"Jake," I said, "there's something that's been worrying me. I don't know if I should tell you..."

"What?" asked David.

"You don't think – is it possible that your dad has a secret girlfriend?"

I had got Jake's attention at last. He stared at me. "You mean he's seeing somebody else, and Mum doesn't know?"

"No," said David at once. "Dad wouldn't do anything like that. Would he?"

"Shut *up*, David," Jake said. "Tell me what makes you think that."

I said, "I've heard your dad on the phone. Talking and laughing. Then when your mum came along, he pretended it was a wrong number. It's happened two or three times that I know of." (Not true, but Jake wouldn't know that.)

"I don't believe you," said David, looking extremely worried.

"I do," said Jake grimly. He went over to the door, making sure it was tightly closed. "Last week I saw him coming out of Susie Milton's house. I thought it was odd at the time – I mean, Susie's one of Mum's friends really, not his."

"Did he say anything?" I asked. "Did he look guilty when he saw you?"

"He never noticed me. I was a long way down the street, but I know it was him. He had this big stupid grin all over his face."

"If he's going out with Susie Milton," said David, "will he and Mum split up? What will happen to us?" His voice trembled.

I felt sorry I'd ever mentioned the phone call, but you can't unsay what's been said. Anyway, if Terry was really cheating on Lisa, maybe it was better that Jake knew about it. He might be able to put a stop to it.

"Who is this Susie person?" I asked.

"She lives round the corner. I think she and Mum went to school together. She owns a clothes shop, so she always dresses pretty smart. You know – like one of those plastic models you see in shop windows."

"She's not as good-looking as Mum, though," said David loyally. "And she has a silly laugh. I don't like her."

"It's not you we're talking about, it's Dad," Jake said. "Listen. From now on we all keep an eye on him, okay? If there really is something going on..." His voice trailed off into silence.

"Yes?" I said. "If there really is something going on, we'll do what?"

"I don't know," said Jake, looking suddenly miserable. "I don't know."

Jake's dad was not the only person with a secret. Henry had one too.

One morning, when he should have been in the kitchen doing the breakfasts, I noticed him out in Reception. He was looking eagerly through the pile of mail that had just arrived. Whatever he was expecting hadn't come, though. He went back to work looking disappointed.

Henry hardly ever got letters. He never talked about friends or family – he was quite a lonely person really. The hotel was his whole life. I wondered what letter he was expecting so eagerly.

The next day, being nosy, I looked through the mail myself. There was a small flat package addressed to Henry. It could have contained a book. The address was on a printed label, which said *Jackson & Co, Reptile Specialists*, in wavy writing like the body of a snake.

"Thank you. I believe that's mine," said Henry, snatching it out of my hand.

I glared at him. "Don't you know it's rude to snatch things?"

"Don't you know it's rude to read other people's mail?" He held the package close to his fat stomach, as if to stop me seeing the label.

"Too late, I've already seen it," I said. "But what's the big secret? Is it a crime to be interested in snakes?"

"Shhh!" he hissed, sounding almost snake-like himself. He looked around nervously, but the hallway was empty.

Rather odd, I thought. But then Henry was a rather odd person. I went off to school and forgot about him completely.

# Chapter 10

## Grace's house

Grace asked me back to her place after school. "Stay for tea, if you like."

"Will Megan be there?" I wanted to know.

"No. She's still off sick… or supposed to be."

"What do you mean? Is she skiving?"

Grace said, "Well, she has been off school a lot this term. She says she feels sick and has a tummy-ache. If it was me saying that all the time, Mum would take me to the doctor, and if there was nothing really wrong she'd make me go back to school."

"Why doesn't Megan's mum do that?"

"I don't know. Too busy with the café, I suppose."

"Does Megan hate school that much, then? Maybe she realises nobody likes her much… except you. But that's her own fault. Nobody likes her because of how she behaves."

Grace gave me a strange kind of look. She said, "I don't think that's why she's been skiving off. I think she does it to keep an eye on her mum."

"Oh. Because she's afraid her mum will run off again?"

"Yes, or her mum and dad will have another huge

row and end up in Casualty."

"Parents!" I said. "They're nothing but trouble." The thought of Megan's parents – and Jake's for different reasons – made me wonder if perhaps I was lucky, just having Mam. In some ways life was easier with only one parent.

Grace's parents were nice, though. Her mum was small and round and smiley, the sort of person you feel at home with straight away. She had a part-time job in a play-group. I could easily imagine her with a child on each knee cuddling up to her while she read a story.

She was busy mixing a cake in the warm, cheerful kitchen. At the other end of the table, Ben was doing his homework. A cat dozed by the cooker, and a small white dog sat hopefully waiting for crumbs to fall on the floor.

"That looks nice, Mum. Can we scrape the bowl out?" asked Grace.

"You can, if you help with the mixing."

"I'd love to," I said eagerly. I never got the chance to do things like that. It was ages since Mam and I had had a kitchen of our own.

Ben looked up. "Mummy, mummy, can I lick the bowl?… No, pull the chain."

"Get out, you disgusting boy," said his mother. "I'm not having jokes like that in my kitchen."

"Oh. You won't like this one, then. Mummy, mummy, why can't we have a dustbin like everybody else has?… Shut up and keep eating."

"Ben! Either do your homework quietly or take it into the dining-room." She said to me, "It's because you're here, Katie. He knows we've heard all his jokes before, but you haven't."

Looking injured, Ben gathered up his books. "Mummy mummy, can I play with Grandad?... For any sake, let Grandad rest in peace. You've dug him up twice this week already."

Grace made being-sick noises. Me – I felt myself shiver slightly, as I always did these days at the thought of death.

"Katie, love, are you all right?" asked Grace's mum.

"Yes, of course I am," I said crossly. "I just felt a bit cold suddenly."

"Come and stir this, then. The exercise will warm you up."

Grace and I worked happily together, stirring cocoa into one half of the cake mixture, then swirling the whole lot together in a tin, so that the finished cake would be a pattern of yellow and brown. I'd seen cakes like that in shops, but I never knew how they were made.

Suddenly Grace said, "Want me to ask her?"

"You what?"

"Ask Mum. To explain about Heaven, and all that."

"Oh, all right."

Grace told her mum about our conversation a few days before. "Read us that bit in the Bible about the wonderful city – you know."

Her mum smiled. She took out a book from beside her cookery books (funny place to keep a Bible, I thought), and opened it near the end. I listened rather wistfully as she read about the city of Heaven.

*... the river of the water of life, sparkling like crystal, flows down the middle of the city's street. On each side of the river is the tree of life, which bears fruit twelve times a year... The throne of God will be in the*

*city, and his people will worship him. They will see his face.*

"And that will be the best thing of all," she said. "Seeing God – seeing his face."

"But what about this bit, Mum?" asked Grace. "You missed out this bit. *Nothing that is under God's curse will be found in the city.*"

Grace's mum said, "That means all the bad things that people do. Hurting each other, stealing, telling lies, feeling proud of themselves… If bad things were allowed into Heaven, quite soon it wouldn't be Heaven any more. It would all be spoiled."

"But everyone does bad things sometimes," I said.

"You're absolutely right, Katie. Nobody's perfect."

"So how does anyone get into Heaven?"

"God doesn't hate us, although he hates the bad things we do. He loves us like a father, and he wants us to be with him in Heaven." She read another bit. *"Only those whose names are written in the Book of the Living will enter the city.* We can all have our names written in that book."

"How?"

"By trusting in God, and telling him we're sorry for the wrong things we've done."

"Is that all?" I thought about it for a minute. Saying sorry – that was easy. But believing in God?

"The trouble is," I said, "I don't believe in God. Whenever I try to, I… I just can't. I don't think there's anybody out there. If there is, I can't imagine what he's like."

"Well, the Bible tells us a lot," said Grace's mum. "It says God is like a loving father – far better than the best of human fathers. He knows all about us. He loves each one of us."

I was silent. That wasn't what *my* father was like. I felt a kind of ache inside me, a huge emptiness that nothing could fill. Because to me, the words "loving" and "father" simply didn't belong together. You might as well talk about "green snow" or "friendly Megan".

"Mum!" Grace cried. "I can smell burning."

"Oh no… the cake!"

We had forgotten it completely. When Grace's mum took it out of the oven, it wasn't brown and yellow, it was brown and black.

Ben came in, sniffing the air. "Knock knock," he said.

"Who's there?" I asked.

"Bernie."

"Bernie who?" I said automatically.

"Bernie toast again? I'll have Corn Flakes."

"Don't encourage him, Katie," said his mum. "Grace, be an angel and set the table for me. We'll have to have ice cream for pudding."

# Chapter 11

## The island

After tea we played Monopoly with Ben. I'd never seen it played before, but I soon got the hang of it. Grace, although she'd played it lots of times, ended up losing. She was too kind-hearted; instead of making people pay when they landed on Mayfair, she kept letting them off.

I got a shock when I looked at the time. Half past eight! "I ought to be going," I said. "Mam will be wondering what's happened to me."

We went up to Grace's bedroom to get my things. It was right at the top of the house. Earlier on, I'd admired the view out across the rooftops of the town, towards the sea. Now darkness had fallen, but in some ways that made the view even better. All the lights of the town were spread out below us; you could see the big wheel at the fun-fair, brightly lit, and a line of coloured lights where the pier stretched out into the dark, empty sea.

Suddenly, far out in the night, a single spot of light appeared and vanished again.

"What was that?" I asked, thinking of ships in danger signalling for help.

"That's the lighthouse on Seal Island," said Grace. "When I was little and felt scared in the night, I always used to look out for it."

"I didn't even know there was an island out there," I said. "You can't see it in daylight, can you?"

"Not the island itself, it's too low and flat. But you can see the lighthouse sticking up, if you know where to look."

Flash – there it was again. Far distant, yet bright and clear, the beam of light gave warning to ships at sea, and comforted children in the darkness.

Grace said, "If you ever get the chance to go out there, it's worth a visit. They do boat trips in summer from the pier. There's a big island – that's where the lighthouse is – and lots of little rocky islands where the seals lie in the sun. Baby seals, too. They're really cute."

"I'd like to see that," I said, wondering if I could ever get Mam into a boat. It would be difficult, but maybe not impossible.

That night, I drew back the curtains of our attic window, which was at least as high up as Grace's room. With luck I should be able to see… ah, there it was. The clear white light stabbed through the darkness, then vanished again.

Strange that there was an island out there which I never knew existed – never even guessed at. It was real, though. Grace had actually seen it. I knew she was a truthful person who didn't make things up, even if she did have some strange ideas about God and all that.

A weird thought came into my mind then. Could it be that Grace was right and I was wrong? That God really was out there, unseen like the island, yet real?

I pressed my face to the cool glass of the window. I sent a silent question out into the night. Are you there, God? Do you really exist? If so… please talk to me.

There was no answer that I could hear. Nothing to see except the flash of the lighthouse far away.

I tried again.

Please, God, if you exist… I would like to know you. Please, please, show me somehow or other that you're real. Oh, and one more thing – please don't let me have that dream again tonight…

Mam came in. "What on earth are you doing, girl? It's a quarter to ten. Into bed with you."

That night I had a dream – but not about road accidents. I dreamed I was out in a boat, all alone under a grey sky. Every time a wave lifted the boat, I scanned the horizon desperately. But there was no sign of land in any direction.

It was scary. The wind was getting stronger, tugging at the sail of my boat. The waves grew bigger and fiercer. I knew that my only hope was to reach land – if there was any land.

That was when I saw the lighthouse. It was small and far away, but against the darkening sky its light shone out again and again. I steered towards it. At last I could see a low green island, as flat as a table-top. Seals swam out towards me as if in welcome, and circled the boat as I brought it in.

I landed safely in a sheltered bay. The boat ran aground on a beach of silver-grey sand. Stepping ashore, I realised that the wind had dropped to a gentle breeze. A break in the clouds showed a glorious sunset.

The island was very peaceful. All I could hear was the lapping of waves, the high-pitched call of seagulls, and the bleating of sheep. There were lots of sheep roaming freely about. The grass they nibbled was as smooth as a lawn, with small white flowers sprinkled over it like stars.

The whole place was so beautiful and quiet and safe, that I didn't mind the fact that night was coming. I knew nothing could hurt me here. If I felt lonely, I would go towards the lighthouse and see who lived there... And then I woke up.

For a few seconds I tried desperately to get back into my dream. It had been so perfect, I didn't want it to end. But I was wide awake by now, and daylight was showing between the curtains.

I ran to the window. It was one of those mornings when mist creeps in from the sea. I couldn't even make out the pier, never mind the distant lighthouse. But I knew it was there all right. Somehow, I was quite sure, I had dreamed about a real place, although I'd never seen it in my life.

And I hadn't had the nightmare about Alice and the car crash. In fact I never had that nightmare again.

I called for Grace on the way to school.

"You look happy," she said. "Is it your birthday or something?"

"Nearly as good. Know something? I didn't get that bad dream last night." (I almost told her about the other dream, but I was afraid that talking about it would spoil the lovely memory.) "And you know why? I think it was because I prayed about it."

"Yes," she said. "I was praying too."

The idea was still so strange, I couldn't get used to it. The idea that God was there, unseen but real – hearing my prayers, knowing my thoughts –

That was the bad part. I didn't want anyone, even God, to know my thoughts, because sometimes they weren't very nice. My thoughts on the inside did not match my face on the outside. If God existed, then he would see all the things I kept hidden from other people.

But if God existed… this was the good part. If God was real – real as the island, strong and secure as the lighthouse – then I would have a safe place to go to whenever things went wrong. I could just pray, and God would make everything all right. Wouldn't he?

In school I sat with my maths book open and my mind far away.

"I do believe in you," I told God silently. "And thank you for the dream. I'll never forget it."

Then, remembering what Grace had said, I added, "And I'm sorry about all the bad things I've done. Especially the lies I've told. From now on I'm only going to tell the truth, I promise."

"Katie!" shouted the teacher. "I've warned you before about day-dreaming. Get on with your work!"

I got on with my work. But all day, during Maths and Music and lunch and Games, a part of my mind was a long way off. On the island.

# Chapter 12

## Something fishy

"Who's been nicking from my fridge again?" shouted Henry. He looked so furious, I didn't risk mentioning that it wasn't actually his fridge. It belonged to the hotel kitchen.

"Own up," he shouted at me. "It was you, you thieving little good-for-nothing. You've been in my fridge!"

"Not me," I said. "I haven't touched your fridge."

"Oh no? What about that big slice of Black Forest Gateau last week?"

"That wasn't me either," I started to say as indignantly as I could. But then I remembered – no more lies. "Er… well, actually that *was* me."

"I knew it!" he roared.

"I haven't taken anything this week, though. I promise."

"You're a little liar. What have you done with my whitebait?"

Jake's mum came hurrying in. "What on earth's the matter, Henry? I could hear you out in Reception. Calm down, will you? If you must shout, shout *quietly*."

"She's nicked my whitebait that I put aside specially!" he said.

"Who has?"

"That one." He couldn't even bring himself to say my name. "Or her mother."

I said, "We don't actually like whitebait." (In case you don't know, whitebait are little fish, smaller than sardines. You can't take the bones out, you have to crunch them up.) "Anyway, how would we cook them? Are you saying we ate them raw?"

"Henry, I'm sure there must be a simple explanation," said Jake's mum. "I expect Terry fried them up for his lunch. He probably thought they were left-overs from last night. I'll ask him when he comes in."

Henry grunted something.

She said, "What did you need them for, anyway? They're not on tonight's menu, are they?"

"No," Henry admitted. "It's prawn cocktail tonight."

I made my escape, wondering why Henry was making such a fuss about a few fish. Black Forest Gateau, now, or profiteroles – I could understand him getting annoyed if those went missing (as they sometimes had in the past, I had to admit). But raw fish?

Five minutes later, Henry came into the games room to see Jake. "Do me a favour, old son. Nip down to the fish stall and get me a pound of whitebait. Make sure they're small ones, mind." He held out some money.

Jake looked reluctant. "You can keep the change," said Henry.

"I'll go," I said eagerly.

"You? I wouldn't trust you with 10p of my money," said Henry scornfully. To Jake he said, "I'd go myself, but I won't have time. There's twenty-five eating in tonight. Go on – I'll cook you whatever you like for your supper."

"Cheeseburger and chips?" said Jake, looking suddenly interested.

Henry sighed. "If that's what you really want."

"Okay then," said Jake.

I followed him out into the street. "Why is Henry so desperate for whitebait? Don't you think it's a bit strange?"

Jake shrugged. "That's Henry for you. He gets these sort of... cravings. He used to eat Polo mints all the time, then he went right off them. Last year it was grapefruit. He was on this grapefruit diet, to lose weight."

"Obviously *that* didn't work," I said.

"No. It might have done, but Dad put a stop to it. Henry was putting grapefruit all over the menu. I mean, people quite like it as a starter, but they're not so keen on grapefruit soup or duck à la grapefruit or grapefruit trifle."

"Better than whitebait soup or whitebait trifle," I said, but Jake wasn't listening.

"Hey!" he said, as we turned the corner into Pump Street. "That's our car."

"So?"

"So what's it doing here?" His voice was sharp. "Dad told Mum he was taking the TV to be mended."

"Oh," I said. "Is this where that woman lives?"

"Yeah – in that house with the green door. I bet he's in there. I just know he is." He aimed a vicious kick at the car tyre.

I said, "We could wait and see if he comes out."

"Yes, but not here. Come round the corner so he doesn't spot us."

We must have looked like a couple of idiots as we stood there, pressed against someone's garden wall, peering round the corner every few seconds. But Jake didn't care. He looked really angry.

"How can he do this to Mum?" he muttered. "I'd like to kill him."

"Steady on. We don't *know* he's seeing that woman. He might be in any of those other houses."

"In that case, why tell lies about mending the TV set? No. He's up to something."

I began to get bored. We'd been waiting for ages; I thought it was time I went back home. But suddenly Jake stiffened. "There he is," he whispered.

When I put my head around the corner, I saw Terry coming down the steps of that house, and the green door closing behind him. He looked sort of... furtive. Yes, that was the word. Furtive and secretive. He got quickly into his car and drove away.

If I hadn't reminded Jake about Henry's fish, he would have forgotten all about them.

"Want me to get them?" I asked, but he said no, he would go. It would give him a chance to think.

"Will you tell your mum?"

"I don't know."

I said, "Don't tell her. She'll only be hurt."

"I know that! Just shut up, Katie. Go home and mind your own business."

"Only trying to help," I said, feeling hurt myself. I didn't speak to Jake again for the rest of the day.

When Henry got his precious whitebait, he didn't

risk leaving them in the hotel fridge. I saw him carry the small, damp parcel down to his flat in the basement. Was he planning to feast on them, raw, in the middle of the night? How weird.

Helping Mam, I had been in and out of every room in the whole hotel – except Henry's. His place was always locked. He did his own cleaning and changed his own sheets. That way he could be sure it was done *properly*, he said.

His flat was in the basement, just along from the games room. If he opened the door, I always tried to steal a glance inside before he quickly closed it again. This annoyed him no end. I had often wondered if he had some deep dark secret hidden in there. The loot from a bank robbery? A year's supply of stolen Polo mints? A dead body?

But now I began to wonder if the secret was… something alive. Something that ate whitebait. Something dangerous, like a snake or an alligator – otherwise, why all the secrecy?

I was determined to find out more. I hoped the secret *was* something dangerous. HOTEL CHEF KEPT CROCODILE IN THE BATH, it would say in the paper. Then Henry would get the sack, and the rest of us would live happily ever after.

# Chapter 13

## Liar, liar

When Megan came back to school, she was very cross that Grace and I had become friends. (What did she expect? Was Grace supposed to talk to no one at all while Megan was off sick?)

During the walk to school, she kept trying to get rid of me. "Get lost, Katie. We don't want you – can't you see that? Just go away."

"I'll go where I like," I said. "You don't own the pavement. You don't own Grace either, come to think of it."

"She's *my* friend, not yours," said Megan angrily.

"I'll go away if Grace tells me to," I offered.

At once Megan said, "Go on. Tell her, Grace."

Grace looked upset. "Look, why can't we all be friends? I like both of you. I don't want to have to choose one or the other."

Secretly I thought that if she was forced to choose, she would pick me. Maybe Megan thought so too. She became even more spiteful.

"You won't catch me being friends with a liar," she said. "You've heard her, Grace – you know the kind of things she says. Her dad's a film star. She's met dozens of famous people and they all told her how pretty she was. Her mum used to work at the Ritz –"

I felt my face go red. "That last one was true. Mam did work at the Ritz when she was young."

"Yeah, as a chambermaid. Big deal!" said Megan. "That's what I can't stand about you, Katie. You're always showing off and you've got nothing to show off about. *And* you're a liar."

"And you're not, I suppose," I said. "You always tell the truth all the time."

"Of course I do."

"Liar yourself. What about pretending to be ill so you can bunk off school? That's not what I'd call one hundred per cent truthful."

She said furiously, "I wasn't pretending. I really had the stomach ache."

"What? Seven times in three weeks? You must be allergic to something. I know – it's school. You're allergic to school, you hate going because nobody likes you and you haven't any friends."

"Oh stop it. Stop it!" said Grace, like a half-trained teacher in a rioting classroom. We hardly heard her.

"Well *you* can't talk," Megan shouted at me. "Nobody likes you either. Nobody believes the lies you tell."

"They do. They like listening to my stories."

"Yeah – so they can laugh at them later, behind your back."

"That's not true," I said.

"Yes it is. I'm right, aren't I Grace?"

Grace looked from one to the other of us. "I wish you'd both stop acting like five-year-olds. If you go on like this, I don't want to be friends with either of you."

And she stalked off into school on her own, leaving us staring after her.

From then on, Megan really started picking on me. A few other people joined in, like Elliot, the American boy, and nasty little Natasha Bacon. But Megan was the ringleader.

Even though I was now trying my best to be truthful, they wouldn't let me forget the things I'd said in the past. They were always going on at me – in the playground, in the classroom, anywhere.

"Today we're going to find out about a famous Roman Emperor," said Mrs Duncan. "He led the invasion of Britain in 55 BC. Does anyone know his name?"

"No, but I expect Katie met him once in Blackpool," Megan muttered, and everyone began sniggering.

In the playground they would crowd around me.

"How's your father the film star? Heard from him lately?"

"The Prime Minister stayed at your hotel last week, didn't he, Katie? Do tell us. Don't be shy."

"Tell us some more of your exciting adventures. Go on, Katie! Tell us about the time when you had to hide up a chimney, and someone lit the fire."

"Liar, liar, pants on fire!"

Grace stood up for me once or twice – but of course that made Megan worse. Soon she started picking on Grace as well. She laughed at her for being a little goody-goody and going to church.

I could see how much that hurt Grace. After all, she had always been a good friend to Megan, even when no one else liked her. And now Megan had turned against her completely. She started walking home with Natasha instead of Grace; they shouted rude things at us in the street.

"Just ignore her," said Grace. "We'll pretend they don't exist."

"Pretend *who* don't exist? I don't see anyone... Nice weather we're having."

"Beautiful," said Grace, although it was raining.

"Liar, liar, pants on fire!" came the chant from across the street.

"It's so unfair," I said. "I'm really trying not to do it any more – tell lies, I mean." (Which wasn't easy. It was a hard habit to break; worse than Mam trying to give up smoking.) "But they always keep on about it. Aren't they ever going to forget what I did?"

"I expect they will in the end. They'll get bored with it," said Grace. "We could pray about it, too."

"I already have." In fact I prayed about it every day on the way to school. Oh, please don't let them pick on me today... "But it doesn't seem to be working," I said gloomily.

"Off to Sunday School again this week, Grace?" Megan shouted. She began to sing a silly version of a hymn. Grace looked upset.

To take her mind off this, I said, "There's something I don't understand. Why do some prayers work and not others?"

"Mmm... I don't really understand that either. We could ask my mum."

We asked her mum.

She said, "That's a very good question. Grown-ups worry about it too. If God really loves us, they say, why doesn't he give us everything we ask for?"

I said, "Have *you* ever prayed about something, but it didn't come true?"

"Oh, yes. There's one person I've prayed about for a long time... years and years."

"And nothing's happened?"

She said, "No. Or maybe I should say, not yet. I'm still asking. We always want things to happen instantly, don't we? We're like little kids. *I want a biscuit and I want it NOW!* But their mum, if she's a good mum, wouldn't give them biscuits all day. It wouldn't be good for them."

Grace said, "You mean, it wouldn't be good for us to get all the things we pray for?"

"That's right. And it certainly wouldn't be good for us to get them straight away. We would turn into spoilt kids, trying to order God about."

I said thoughtfully, "But if some prayers are answered and some not, then what's the point? I mean, why bother praying at all?"

Grace's mum took her Bible from the kitchen shelf. "Look, I read this only this morning. *The Lord is near to those who call to him.* Doesn't matter whether the answer to our prayer is 'yes' or 'no' or 'yes, but not yet'... whenever we pray, he is near to us."

Then she said briskly, "But another thing we must remember is, not only to pray but to do our part as well. I'm very glad you told me about the situation with Megan. If it goes on, I'll have a word with your teacher, shall I?"

# Chapter 14

## David and Goliath

"Katie!" shouted Jake. "Phone."

I hurried downstairs, four flights from the attic, wondering who it was. Nobody ever phoned me.

"Hello, Katie," came the smooth voice of Mrs Parkes. "How would you like to take another little trip this Sunday?"

My heart sank. "Oh, do I have to? Can't I pay you the money instead? I've nearly saved up enough…"

"No, dear. We had an agreement. One more trip and then she's yours, all yours. Are you busy on Sunday?"

"In the morning I am," I said. (Grace had invited me to church with her). "I could come at about twelve – is that any good?"

"Very well. That will still give us time for what I have in mind," she said.

What was I going to tell Mam? I didn't want to lie to her, and yet I didn't want to spoil the surprise, either. Luckily she assumed that I would be going to Grace's house after church and having lunch there. These days I was spending a lot of time at Grace's.

The church service was a surprise. I hadn't been to one for years and years – not since my Nan died. She used to take me to church sometimes. I remembered it as a cold and gloomy place, smelling of dampness, furniture polish, and the toffees Nan gave me to keep me quiet.

Grace's church was quite different. The music was lively, with drums and guitars. But I couldn't join in the singing because I didn't know any of the songs. After a while all the children went out to a room at the back. A lady played an out-of-tune piano and we sang some more. Then we had a sort of mini-RE lesson about David and Goliath.

Although it wasn't as deadly boring as my Nan's church, where the sermon used to seem about ten hours long, I couldn't honestly say I had enjoyed it. I hoped Grace wouldn't expect me to go every week – I had better things to do.

"Do you *have* to go to church on Sundays?" I asked Grace's mum as we came out. "I mean, can't people believe in God and not go to church?"

"Of course they can. But most people find that it helps them. It's not easy being a Christian all on your own."

"Oh." (But I'm not on my own, I told myself. I've got Grace and her family to help me.)

Grace's mum said, "And it's amazing how often I hear something in church that's exactly what I need. God can speak to us through the songs, or the sermon, or the Bible readings – he really can."

I didn't think I'd heard God speak to me that morning. But maybe I hadn't been listening very hard.

"Oh! You've had your hair cut," said Mrs Parkes. She looked put out.

"Don't you like it? I didn't at first, but I've got used to it."

"Well, it suits you, I suppose. It's very… modern, though. And couldn't you have put on a dress? Old people often think jeans are rather scruffy."

I didn't care. I just wanted to get the trip over with, and collect my flower girl.

"Where are we going?" I asked.

"Not far from where we were before. Different villages, of course."

At first things went well. It was a lovely day; lots of people were out in their gardens, enjoying the sun. This made it easy for Mrs Parkes to get chatting to them. I hardly ever had to ask them for a drink.

Mrs Parkes bought quite a lot of things – two clocks, a small table, a silver tea-pot, a set of plates. A deaf old lady sold her several ornaments, including another flower girl just like my one, for fifty pounds.

"Look at this, Katie! You could have a matching pair. Come out on two more trips with me and I'll give you this one. How about it? I really think you bring me luck, you know."

"I don't need two flower girls," I said. "My Nan only had one."

We had a late lunch in the garden of a pub. "Choose whatever you like, dear," said Mrs Parkes. "I'll treat you." She was being ever so nice to me, which made me feel guilty, because I couldn't like her however hard I tried.

We moved on to another village, where we bought a few more bits and pieces. But now she began looking at her watch. "Mustn't spend too long here. There's one more place I want to visit. Do you remember the old man who thought he knew us?"

I stood quite still.

"Oh no," I said. "I'm not doing that again. I'm not having those dreams again... and anyway I've stopped telling lies."

She laughed. "You *are* a funny girl, Katie. Whatever do you mean? Come on, hop in the car and tell me about it as we go along."

So I explained about the car crash, and Alice who had haunted my dreams. I told her we had been impersonating two dead people.

But she didn't seem to care. "In a way that makes it even better," she said. "I was rather worried that his real family might turn up while we were there! Just think... they've been dead for years and the old chap doesn't realise. He must be completely batty."

She had that greedy look on her face again. She was probably planning what else she could take from the poor, confused old man.

"I won't do it," I said. "I won't go in there. You can't make me."

"Oh, can't I?" Her hands gripped the steering wheel so tightly that the knuckles went white. "You'll do as I say, miss. Or else you can get out of the car right now and find your own way home."

Did she really mean it? We were miles and miles from Westhaven. I had no idea how to get back there, and no money. What would I do if she dumped me here, right out in the country, miles from anywhere? No one, including me, would have a clue where I was.

But then I remembered – there was someone who did know where I was.

Oh God, please help me. I'm dead scared, I don't

know what to do... Help me!

Was this how David felt when he saw the giant Goliath stamping up and down? David was only a boy; his enemy was bigger and meaner and tougher than he was. Like Mrs Parkes, who was bigger and meaner and tougher than me.

Suddenly I felt glad that I'd been to church that morning. The story of David was just what I needed to know. David, of course, had won in the end, by trusting in God and doing his best with the few weapons he had. Big strong Goliath was totally defeated.

Feeling braver – just a little bit – I sat silently as we drove through the country lanes. At last we came to a village I had seen before and a house I knew. The car stopped.

"Out you get, Alice," said Mrs Parkes. "Grandfather will be *so* pleased to see us again."

# Chapter 15

## Spider web

"You've forgotten about my hair," I said. "I don't look like Alice any more. She had long fair hair – I saw it in the photos."

Mrs Parkes looked annoyed, but not for long. "I don't suppose it matters much," she said. "The old chap's quite dotty; he'll believe whatever we tell him. Just pretend to be Alice, like you did last time, and he won't suspect a thing."

I shook my head. "I told you – I've stopped telling lies."

"How very commendable." Her smile was more like a snarl. "But you won't have to tell any lies, if that's how you feel. Just say nothing at all. I'll do the talking."

"No. I'm not going to pretend I'm somebody else." That would still be dishonest, I knew. Even if I never opened my mouth, I would be acting out a lie.

"Then you can say goodbye to the flower seller."

"That's not fair!" I cried. "I've earned her – you said so!"

"Don't you take that tone with me, madam," she said in a voice like a knife-blade. "*You* don't make the rules – I do. Now get out of the car."

"No."

For a second I thought she was going to hit me. I said, "If you make me go in there, I'll yell my head off. There are people in hearing distance – do you want them all to know what you're doing?"

She stared at me. Her eyes, narrowed like a cat's, were full of fury and hatred.

"Very well," she said at last. "I don't need you anyway, you stupid child. I can do it without you. Just wait in the car."

I sank back, feeling weak with relief. I watched her go up the path and knock on the door. Don't answer it! Don't let her in!

But he did. I heard him cry, "Joan, my dear! They tried to tell me you wouldn't come back, but somehow I knew you would. Where's little Alice?"

"She's at school, Daddy. She sends you her love."

Then they went in, and the door was shut.

What should I do now? I really didn't want Mrs Parkes to get away with it. If she did, she would keep on coming back until the old man had nothing left that was worth taking. But how could I stop her? I didn't know anyone round here, and the village looked too small to have a police station.

All at once I heard voices from a neighbouring garden.

"It's the same car, I'm sure of it."

"Different child, though. The other one had fair hair."

"But the woman called him 'Daddy'. You heard her. She's passing herself off as Frank's daughter!"

An elderly man and woman were staring at me over

their hedge. My first instinct was to cower down so that they couldn't see me. But then I thought, wait a minute… maybe they can help.

Hoping that Mrs Parkes wasn't looking out of the window, I got out of the car. I stood where the hedge would hide me if she did look out.

"You're right," I said to the elderly couple. "She is pretending to be his daughter. She wanted me to help her but I wouldn't."

"I knew it!" said the old lady. "Ring the police, Desmond. Quickly! You know how long it takes them to get out here from town."

Her husband hurried indoors. I began to panic. What would Mrs Parkes say when she knew what I'd done? Should I get back in the car and pretend I had been there all the time?

"Don't be frightened, dear," said the old lady. "Come indoors and wait with us until the police come. We'll take care of you. Who is that woman, anyway? Not your mummy, I hope."

"She's just someone I know," I said. "She has an antique shop in Westhaven." As I said it, I remembered the flower girl. Mam would never get her birthday present now, would she?

Then I thought of the other flower girl – the one we'd bought earlier in the day. It was in the boot of the car, in a box; I knew exactly where. Cautiously I opened the boot, took out the ornament, and closed the door again as quietly as I could. Then I fled into the neighbours' garden.

It was all right – Mrs Parkes didn't come out. Probably all her attention was on the old man and his treasures.

"Do come inside," said the old lady. "Desmond has rung the police. All we have to do now is wait. Would you like a cup of tea or a glass of water?"

"No thanks."

We waited for ages. I listened hopefully for the sound of a siren, but all I heard was the buzzing of bees outside the window. It was a very quiet street. A couple of cars passed by; one drew in further along the road. But it wasn't a police car.

"If they don't come soon, it will be too late," I said.

"I'm afraid it's often like this," the old man said. "They have to come all the way from Gullford. It's the price we pay for living in the country."

Then I heard a door closing and feet crunching on the gravel path next door. Cautiously we looked out from behind the net curtains. Mrs Parkes was heading for her car, with two large vases in her arms.

"Oh no," I groaned. "Too late... she's getting away."

Suddenly, in the car that was parked along the road, all the doors opened at once. Four policemen came running to surround Mrs Parkes as she stood by her car. Her face went as white as a piece of bone china.

"Aha!" cried Desmond. "They were waiting to catch her with the evidence. It's a fair cop – they got her bang to rights."

"Desmond, you've been watching too much television," said his wife disapprovingly.

We watched as Mrs Parkes handed over the vases and her car keys. She was put in the back of the other car and driven away.

"Good riddance," said the old lady.

"I only hope Frank didn't see it," her husband said.

"His daughter being arrested! Still, I don't suppose he would remember it for long."

The old couple, Desmond and Daisy Fox, took me back all the way to Westhaven in their car. It was very kind of them.

They explained that they liked to keep an eye on Frank, their neighbour. "His mind, you see… it's not what it was." They had noticed two strangers, a girl and a woman, visiting him a couple of weeks before. When they popped in to see Frank, and found that one of his pictures was missing, they informed the police. But they were told that there was little hope of catching the thieves.

"The police said they would be miles away by then, and unlikely to come back. So we could hardly believe it when we saw her again," said Daisy.

Desmond said, "I wonder who that girl was, the one with the long fair hair? She was obviously in on the whole thing. Maybe the police will manage to track her down."

I felt as if I'd been kicked in the stomach. I knew I ought to say something… I ought to tell them the truth. But somehow I couldn't do it.

The old lady said, "I didn't get a proper look at her. Nicely dressed, I remember that. Long hair in an Alice band. About the same height as you, dear, but younger-looking. Do you know her?

"No. No, I don't. Mrs Parkes did mention a niece once…"

"I expect we'll have to make a statement to the police," said Desmond. He sounded as if he rather liked the idea – but it sent me into a panic. What if he told the police about me, and I had to make a statement too?

I decided it would be safer not to let Desmond and Daisy find out where I lived. Instead of Sea View, I directed them to Grace's house on the opposite side of the square.

The trouble with telling lies is, there's no end to it. You can never tell just *one* lie. Like a fly trapped in a spider's web, you get more and more tangled in the sticky threads.

When Daisy said, "I've just realised, dear, we don't even know your name," I said I was called Megan.

"Megan – what a pretty name. And your surname?"

"Bacon." It was the first name that came to mind, but as I said it I felt my face grow red. Megan Bacon! Like one of Ben's dreadful jokes. When Daisy thought about it, she'd be sure to realise it was a made-up name.

She didn't seem to notice, though. As we pulled up outside Grace's house, she said, "Shall I come in and explain things to your mother, Megan?"

"Oh! No, you mustn't," I said hastily. "My mum doesn't know where I went today. I only went out with Mrs Parkes so that I could have this ornament – it's a surprise for Mam's birthday." (At least that part was true.)

Daisy looked at me doubtfully. "Are you sure, dear? All right then. Look, here's our phone number if you need to get in touch." She wrote it down for me.

"Goodbye," I said, "and thank you for bringing me back."

Grace answered the door to me, looking surprised. "Er… we're just having tea."

"Can I come in for a minute?" I waved goodbye to Desmond and Daisy as I closed the door. "I just wanted to ask if you could look after this for me. It's for Mam's birthday, and I've got nowhere to hide it in our bedroom."

"Oh... isn't it lovely?" said Grace.

The flower girl *was* pretty, but I had lost all pleasure in her. Instead of reminding me of Nan, she now made me think of Mrs Parkes and the confused old man. Of lies, trickery and pretence.

My Nan didn't like lies. "Tell the truth and shame the devil," I remembered her saying. She wouldn't think much of the things I'd said in the car – one lie after another. But Nan was dead. And no one else need ever know.

Except God. He knew...

I didn't want to think about that. God had helped me to defeat a strong enemy, and how had I thanked him? By breaking my promise not just once but several times.

It was useless to think I could ever be any different. I was a liar and I would always be a liar, however hard I tried to change.

# Chapter 16

## Something out of nothing

Jake asked for my help! I was pleased.

"What do you want me to do?"

He said, "Help me keep an eye on Dad. If you see him go out, tell me so I can follow him."

"What if you're not around – should I follow him myself?"

Jake looked uncertain. "You could do… as long as you're careful not to be seen. Just go to the corner and find out if he goes to that woman's house or not. If not, then you needn't follow him any further."

But nothing happened for several days. Terry went out now and then; Jake followed him four times. Each time he walked right past the house with the green door, hardly even looking at it.

"Maybe he's stopped seeing her," I said to Jake.

"Or maybe he goes there while we're in school," said Jake gloomily. "Another thing – he's started looking through the mail as soon as it arrives. He never used to do that."

"You think he's expecting a letter from *her*?"

"Yeah, and he doesn't want Mum to see it."

I said, "Why would she write him letters if she only

lives around the corner?"

He shrugged. "People do strange things when they're in love."

"Have *you* ever been in love, Jake?" I asked hopefully.

"Me? No way," he said. "I've got better things to do."

One day, as I crossed the Square on my way home from school, I saw Terry going out again. Jake was nowhere in sight, so it was up to me. And this time, as I peered round the corner into Pump Street, I struck lucky. Or unlucky.

Terry knocked on the green door, looking up and down the street as if he was anxious about being seen. Quickly I drew back around the corner. When I looked again, very cautiously, he was just going into the house.

I smiled to myself. Jake would be pleased with me.

As I turned to go back, I glanced across the street at the Corner Café, and saw someone watching *me*. Instantly her head went down and she started wiping a dirty table-top. Too late, though – I'd seen her.

Why was Megan hard at work in her dad's café, when she hadn't been in school for the last two days? I ran across and tapped on the window.

"Hey, Megan! Thought you were supposed to be ill. I'm going to tell the teacher you've been bunking off."

Megan made a rude sign at me and carried on working. She didn't actually look too healthy, now that I saw her properly. In fact she looked exhausted. Had she been on her feet in the café all day?

In a seaside town, hotels and cafés are quiet all winter and frantically busy all summer. It was June now, the run-up to the busy season. Probably, when school broke up, Megan would have to help in the café. But she shouldn't be missing school to do it. I could get her into trouble for that... big trouble.

Thinking about this, I nearly bumped into Jake.

"Jake! Your dad – I just saw him go to that house again."

If I was expecting thanks, I was disappointed. His face looked hard and grim. "Right. I'm going to wait until he comes out, and then tell him he's got to stop seeing her. Or else."

"Or else what?"

"Or else I'll tell Mum."

I said, "Oh, Jake, be careful. Are you sure that's the best thing to do?"

"No, but I can't think of anything better. Can you?"

I would have gone with him, but he wouldn't let me. "Go home, Katie. This is private between me and Dad."

He didn't come back for ages. When he did come round the corner, I was amazed to see that his dad was with him, and they were both laughing. Jake looked happier than he had been for ages.

As soon as I got the chance, I asked Jake what had happened.

"It was all a mistake," he said. "We got it all wrong. He's not going out with Susie at all."

I stared at him. "Then why does he keep going round to see her?"

"That's a secret."

"Oh come on! I did help you, didn't I? You can trust me. I won't tell anyone, not even David."

"Especially not David," said Jake. "He's useless at

keeping secrets. Anyway, he'll know soon enough. What's happening is, it's Mum's birthday next week – her fortieth. She keeps saying she hates the idea of being 40 and she doesn't want to celebrate. So Dad and Susie are planning a surprise party to cheer her up."

"Ah! So that's the reason for the secret phone calls."

"Yes, and that's why he was checking through the mail. People were supposed to address their replies to Susie, but one or two, like idiots, sent them here."

"So it's all okay," I said. "All that worry for nothing."

"Yes." He grinned a huge grin. "Sounds like it's going to be quite a party. They've invited sixty people."

"Where's it going to be?"

"Here."

I didn't understand. How could they possibly get ready, in secret, for a party of sixty? Jake's mum was bound to see what was going on.

He said, "Oh, she knows there's going to be a party – she just doesn't realise it's for her. She thinks it's for the Bowling Club. Somehow or other we've got to get her out of the way while all the guests arrive. Otherwise she'll think it's rather odd that all her friends and relatives have taken up bowling."

I suddenly felt envious. Compared to this, Mam's birthday would be a very quiet affair. She didn't have six friends, let alone sixty.

"You and your mum are invited, of course," said Jake. "Henry, too."

The mention of Henry reminded me of something. I told Jake what I suspected about Henry's interest in reptiles. "And remember when he sent you out for whitebait? I bet it wasn't for him – it was for his pet, whatever it is. An anaconda or an alligator or something."

Jake laughed. "Oh, Katie. You're doing it again – making something out of nothing."

"Are you saying I'm a liar?" I said angrily.

"Well, you sometimes exaggerate a bit. Don't you? Just to make life more exciting. I mean, it was you that got me all worked up about Dad and his phone calls."

"It wasn't my fault!" I cried. "I was telling the truth then. And I am now."

"Yeah, yeah. David's told me some of the things you've been saying at school. You've got a great imagination, Katie."

I was boiling with fury. "I am not making this up! Listen, what would it take to make you believe me?"

"Seeing this alligator, or whatever, with my own eyes."

"Okay," I said, and began to make my plans.

# Chapter 17

## Make a difference

It wouldn't be at all easy to get into Henry's flat. Mam didn't have a key for it, but there must be a spare key somewhere. I vaguely remembered seeing an enormous key-ring, with about thirty keys on it, somewhere in the office. If I could borrow that just for ten minutes… and of course I would have to be sure that Henry was out of the way…

I had a brilliant idea. The party! Everyone would be busy, especially Henry – a buffet meal for sixty would mean a lot of hard work. And the office would be empty. (Locked, of course, but Mam had a key so that she could get in there to clean. I knew exactly where she kept it.)

If Jake and I slipped away for a few minutes, no one would miss us. Ten minutes, that's all we would need. Get the key, open the door, find the mysterious creature, lock the door again. Henry would never suspect a thing.

And Jake would be sorry he'd ever called me a liar.

It was only a couple of weeks until the school play. Mrs Duncan was getting annoyed with the people who hadn't learned their lines. One of these was Megan. Not only did she forget what to say, she forgot where to come in, what to do – everything.

"Megan! I know you've missed several rehearsals, but that's no excuse for not even trying. Now that you *are* here, I want you to concentrate really hard. Megan, are you listening?" Mrs Duncan rapped on the stage with a stick, and Megan jumped as if she'd been hit.

"She looks really tired," Grace whispered.

Megan seemed almost asleep standing up. Back in the classroom, she actually did fall asleep with her head on the desk. (Not that I blamed her – we were still doing the boring old Roman Empire.)

Mrs Duncan said, "I'm going to write a note to your parents, Megan. I really think you ought to see a doctor."

Round at Grace's house after school, I said, "I know why Megan's so tired these days. I saw her working in the café the other day when she was supposed to be off sick. She was in there this morning, too – rushing around like crazy, clearing tables."

"Oh. Maybe her mum's gone off again," said Grace.

"Who?" said Grace's mum, as she stitched away at Grace's costume for the play. "Megan's mum, are you talking about? No, she's still around. I saw her today coming out of the doctor's."

"Is she ill?"

"Not *ill* exactly, unless you count morning sickness. She's expecting a baby."

Grace said, "Really? Megan never told me. Mind you, she doesn't talk to me much these days."

"She doesn't talk to anyone much these days," I said. "She's too tired. But who's complaining? At least she's stopped picking on us."

Grace's mum said, "Poor Megan. No wonder she looks exhausted, if she's trying to take her mum's place in the café. That's a long old day, breakfast through to suppertime. I don't know what her parents are thinking of, letting her do it."

Suddenly she remembered something. "Oh, talking of Megan – she hasn't been here recently, has she?"

"No, why?"

"It's just that someone called, asking for a girl called Megan, and insisting that she lived here. I said the only Megan I knew of lived at the Corner Café."

I had that awful feeling again, like a punch in the stomach – the feeling of my past catching up with me.

"Who was asking? Was it the police?" I asked, trying not to sound as scared as I felt.

"The police?" Grace's mum looked surprised. "No, it was an elderly lady. She was quite definite that she'd seen this girl Megan come in here on Sunday afternoon."

"And why did she want to see her?" I almost whispered.

"She wanted to return a jumper that the girl had left at her house. That's what she said, anyway. It all sounded rather odd to me."

So that was where my red jumper had gone. I knew it had been missing since Sunday; I must have taken it off in Daisy's house while we waited for the police to come. For a moment I felt relieved.

But what if the jumper was just an excuse? Perhaps Daisy had really called so that she could check up on me. And now she would know I'd given her a false name and address. What must she be thinking about me now?

It was goodbye to my jumper – that was for sure. When Mam noticed I'd lost it, I'd better have a good story ready for her. Lies, more lies...

Grace was looking at me rather oddly. She had probably guessed that the Megan of Sunday afternoon was really me. But I knew I could trust her not to say anything in front of her mum. Grace was good like that.

Even when we were alone, up in her room, she didn't ask awkward questions. She just waited for me to tell her, if I wanted to. And by that time I did want to. In fact I was desperate to tell someone the whole story.

When I had spilt it all out like dirty dishwater, I expected her to be shocked. But she wasn't. She said, "Why are you feeling so bad? *You* weren't the one who stole things, it was Mrs Parkes."

"I helped her, though," I said gloomily.

"Only when you didn't know what she was doing. As soon as you realised, you stopped helping her."

"Yes, but will the police believe that?"

Grace said, "The old couple will tell them. They saw you. They know you didn't go into the house."

"Oh... but I told them all those lies! They probably don't trust me any more. They'll think I must have done something wrong, or why would I give them a false name?"

I stared miserably out of the window. It would have been far better to tell the truth, however scared I felt at the time. I saw that now – but it was too late.

In the gathering dusk, a spark of light leapt out and was gone. The lighthouse! But the sight of it was no comfort. I could not picture the island any more, or imagine landing my boat on the silver sand. I would spoil the peace and beauty of the place. I was a liar, I would always be a liar...

"It's no good," I said. "I did try, but I just can't do it."

"Can't do what?"

"Stop telling lies. It's no good, I'm useless... God must really hate me."

"No!" said Grace. "Don't talk like that! Of course God doesn't hate you. Even when you do something really terrible, if you come back to God and tell him you're sorry, then it's all right."

"How do *you* know?" I said bitterly. "It's easy for you. You're always so good, you've never done anything terrible."

She went quite pink. "I know because it says so in the Bible. I don't know where exactly... Mum will know."

We went down to the kitchen, where Grace's mum was ironing her costume. "Oh, those ears," she moaned. "I'm never going to get them right. Why couldn't you be a person instead of a rabbit, Grace?"

I said, "Mine's even worse. I'm supposed to be a squirrel with a long bushy tail. Mam says I can be the world's first tailless squirrel."

When Grace told her what I wanted to know, her mum switched off the iron with a sigh of relief. She read us the story of the son who went away from home and wasted all the money his father had given him, and then was afraid to go back. But at last he did decide to go home and tell his father he was sorry.

"Do you think his father turned him away?" asked Grace's mum.

"I don't know," I muttered.

She said, "His father saw him coming when he was far down the road, ran to him, and threw his arms around him. 'Father, I'm sorry –' the son said. But the father was shouting, 'Bring out the best food, we'll have a party! Look! My son who was lost has been found!'

"Jesus told us that story to show us how much God loves us. Like that father who came running out to meet his son, he loves us so much that whenever we come back to him –"

"What, every time?" I interrupted. "Even if we keep on doing it?"

"Well, yes… if we're really sorry. But what's the problem?"

I told her how hard it was for me to keep telling the truth. "It's like I've got used to telling lies. We did it for years, Mam and me."

"Yes, I understand," she said. "It's very hard to change – like trying to lift yourself up in the air by your own shoelaces. But there *is* a way to be different."

"How?" I asked.

"By letting God change us from the inside. When we trust in him, he gives us his Holy Spirit to be with us always. To help us."

She picked up the sleeve she had been ironing. When she let go it flopped down lifeless and limp. "Look – that's what it's like when we try to do things on our own. We're weak; there's no strength in us. But now, see what happens when someone puts it on."

When Grace put her arm in the sleeve, naturally it wasn't weak and floppy any more. It was strong. It could carry things without bending.

"Do you see what I mean?" said Grace's mum. "With God's Holy Spirit living inside us, we can be strong. We can do the things God wants us to do. We can be the kind of people he wants us to be."

I still felt confused. She must have seen it in my face.

"Maybe we should pray about this," she said. "If you want to, that is."

I nodded; she put her arm round me. "Dear Father, thank you for giving us your Holy Spirit to change us from the inside. Thank you that Katie is your child, and she wants to obey you. Please give her truth instead of lies and courage instead of fear. Amen."

I opened my eyes and looked around. I didn't *feel* any different – any braver or more truthful. Had the prayer been answered? I would just have to wait and see.

# Chapter 18

## Half asleep

Next day, Megan was late for school; she was panting as if she'd run all the way. Mrs Duncan told her off, but she hardly seemed to hear. When she pushed past me to get to her seat, I caught the smell of the café on her clothes. It wasn't the world's most appetizing smell – a mixture of greasy chips, fried onions and stale cigarette smoke.

The normal thing for me to do would have been to hold my nose as she went past, or say something catty. Today, though, I kept quiet. I found myself almost feeling sorry for her, she looked so tired and fed up.

At break I noticed her again. She was sitting in a corner, all alone. Without the wall she was leaning on, she looked as if she would have had trouble staying upright. Her head flopped down on her chest; her arms were as limp as old lettuce.

I nudged Grace. "Look at Megan. Do you think she's okay?"

Grace made a move towards her, then hesitated. I knew what she was thinking – Megan might turn nasty on her. It would be safer to leave her alone.

"We could tell Mrs Duncan," I said.

"How would that help? She'll only go on about Megan seeing a doctor. I don't think she likes Megan much."

"Can you blame her?" I muttered. But all the same I followed Grace over to the corner where Megan sat staring at the ground.

Grace sat down beside her and touched her gently on the arm. "Megan? Are you all right?"

Megan didn't answer, so she asked her again. "Are you okay? Don't you feel well?"

"Go away," Megan mumbled. "Leave me alone."

I wondered if she was on drugs, or drunk maybe, like the people I'd seen lying huddled under the arches by the station. Surely not – she was only ten.

Grace said, "I'll go away if you want me to. But first of all, will you tell me what's wrong?"

"Nothing. I'm tired, that's all." She gave an enormous yawn; I could see all her fillings.

"Tired because of working in the café?" Grace asked, and Megan nodded. "Is it because your mum doesn't feel too good?"

"Yeah. She's having a baby. She gets that, what's it's name, morning sickness. Keeps wanting to throw up."

Not surprising, I thought, if she had to work in the Corner Café. The greasy smells would make anyone want to throw up, pregnant or not.

"So she's making you do her work for her?" said Grace.

"Not *making* me! I wanted to help," said Megan. "Anything to shut him up, I thought."

"Shut who up – your dad?" I said.

Normally Megan would have told me to clear off

and mind my own business. Today she didn't have the energy. She simply nodded.

Grace said, "I suppose they've started having rows again."

"Yeah. Dad doesn't want another baby," Megan said in a dreary voice. "He keeps saying we can't afford it. Another mouth to feed, and how can he run the café on his own? He says she should get rid of it, get it adopted. So then she tries to get up and serve the breakfasts, but she has to keep rushing out to be sick. She looks terrible…"

"So you said you'd do it instead of her," said Grace.

"Mum tells me if I can do the breakfasts, she can manage the rest. She doesn't feel so bad later on in the day, see. But often, by the time I get finished, it's too late to come to school, because I'll only get in trouble for being late. So Dad writes me a sick note."

Grace said, "If you go on missing school, you'll be in worse trouble. Well, not you – your mum and dad. Can't they get someone else in to help?"

"Dad tried to. But we can't pay as much as the hotels, and there are loads of hotel jobs going, so who'd want to work for us?"

"What about your brother – why can't he help?" I said.

"He's got a paper round in the mornings. Anyway, he's useless. Always dropping plates and spilling things, and Dad gets mad, and yells at him."

I thought Megan's dad didn't sound like the nicest person in the world to work for, but I said nothing.

Grace said, "You can't go on like this for ever, Megan. You'll get sick too, and that won't help anybody."

Megan said, "It isn't for ever. Only until Mum gets over the morning sickness."

"And how long will that take?"

"Don't know," she mumbled. "Few more weeks. But I'm so tired..." Her eyelids began to close.

Grace looked at me helplessly. Perhaps the kindest thing would be to let her get some sleep... But then the bell rang for the end of break. Megan gave a little moan and got slowly to her feet, like a weary animal when it hears the crack of the whip.

After school, Grace told me her crazy idea. "Only if Mum lets me," she said.

"You're mad," I said. "You actually *want* to get up at half past six and work for two hours, and then come to school smelling like a chip pan?"

"Not exactly want to. But I do want to help Megan. Of course, I may not be any good at it – I've never done it before."

I told her the things I'd learned from helping at Sea View. Clear the tables as soon as you can, because customers hate sitting in front of some one else's cold leftovers. Always serve people in the order they came in, or they get really mad. Apologise if they have to wait. Be polite to everyone, and above all – even if you hate them – smile!

"I'll try to remember," she said doubtfully.

Next morning, when I called for Grace, her mum looked rather worried. "She's still over at the café, and she hasn't even got her school uniform on yet. At this rate she's going to be late for school."

"I'll tell her to come back, shall I?"

I ran over to the café. "Grace, your mum says to go

home and get changed."

"I can't, not yet," said Grace. "We're not nearly finished."

Looking round, I saw she was right. There were impatient customers waiting to be served, and all the empty tables were piled with dirty plates and cups. I sighed.

"I'll do a bit while you get ready for school," I said, and she gave me a grateful look. Even Megan looked pleased! I couldn't believe it.

As fast as I could, I stacked the dishwasher and switched it on (which neither of them seemed to have thought of in their hurry). Then I cleared and wiped the tables, while Megan took the remaining orders.

Behind the counter, in a sweaty haze, her dad worked away, frying plate after plate of sausage, bacon, egg and tomato. He never said a word to me, but after a while I heard him say to Megan, "She's good, that one. Knows what she's doing without being told. The other one was a waste of time."

Waste of time – was he talking about Grace? I felt pleased that there was something, however small, that I could do better than Grace could. (But then it was only thanks to Grace that I was here at all.)

She came hurrying back, dressed for school. "Is there much more to do?" she panted.

"No," said Megan. "That's the rush over with now. It will be quiet now till lunch-time."

"Thanks, girls," said Megan's dad. He gave us each a couple of quid from the till. "You did a great job," he said, looking at me.

"Yeah – thanks," said Megan awkwardly. No *sorry I picked on you*. No *forgive me for being so mean*. This was Megan we were dealing with. Saying thanks was the best she could do.

"Come on," said Grace. "If we run, we can just about make it to school in time."

I told Mam to wake me up early next day; I was going to help in the café. She didn't like the idea at first, but I explained it was a sort of emergency. At last she said, "All right. You can try it for a week and see how it goes."

As Grace got better at the job, the three of us made a good team. Usually we managed to serve the breakfast, clear up, and still get to school on time. Megan stopped looking so tired. She was almost her normal self again, but with a difference… she didn't seem to hate me any more.

Now and then Megan's mum looked in, as pale as a ghost. "Go back to bed, Mum," Megan would tell her. "And don't worry. We can manage."

# Chapter 19

## Happy birthday

At Sea View we were all getting geared up for the secret birthday party. Lisa was hurrying around, setting out extra chairs in the lounge, counting out glasses and cutlery, and reminding all the residents that the dining room would be closed after eight o'clock for a special function. She had no idea that the special function was all for her.

David told me, "She thinks Dad forgot her birthday. When I gave her my present this morning, he pretended to look guilty, as if he'd suddenly remembered. She got really mad."

"How are you going to get the guests here without her noticing?" I asked.

"That's down to me," he said, looking important. "I'm going to Matthew's house after school. They live miles away, in Little Mardow. Matthew's mum is supposed to be bringing me back, but she's going to ring Mum and tell her the car's broken down, so Mum has to come and fetch me."

"And you've got to act normal all the way home," I said.

"Huh!" said Jake. "David acting normal? No chance."

Over at Ben's house, we had made a huge banner saying LISA IS 40. It was wide enough to go right across the lounge, with bright red lettering edged in glitter-glue.

"I don't think she's going to like this, you know," Jake said.

"Why not? I think it's great," I said.

"I'm not talking about the banner. I mean, she won't like everyone knowing she's hit the big four-O. She's been fibbing about her age for years. If people ask, she says she's thirty-five."

I said, "I don't understand why grown-ups want people to think they're younger than they really are. It's pointless."

"I bet you do the same, when you grow up," said Jake.

"I bet I don't. I'm going to tell them the truth." I said it quite confidently, because when Grace's mum prayed for me, it seemed to have worked. Amazing! I hadn't told a single lie, fib, falsehood or untruth for several days. I had hardly even wanted to.

When we took the rolled-up banner across to Sea View, Lisa happened to see us coming in. "Whatever have you got there?" she asked.

I said, "Oh, just a bit of artwork." (Which was perfectly true.) A harmless fib came to mind: why not pretend it's for school? Luckily, before I needed to say any more, someone rang the bell at Reception, and Lisa hurried off.

"Phew!" said Jake. "That could have been tricky. Where can we hide this until tonight?"

"How about in the games room? Your mum hardly ever goes there."

"Yeah. Under the snooker table – she absolutely

never goes there."

When we passed Henry's door, I remembered my plan of action.

"Jake," I whispered, "where does your dad keep that big key-ring, with a key for every door in the place?"

"In the office, of course. I think it's usually in the desk – the top right-hand drawer. Why do you want to know?"

"Because I'm going to take a look inside Henry's place. Tonight, while the party's going on. Want to come?"

"Are you nuts?" said Jake. "He'll go totally mad if he catches you in there."

"He's not going to catch me. He'll be far too busy at the party. I want to see what sort of reptile he's keeping as a pet."

"Oh, you're not still on about that, are you? Listen, Henry would never keep a snake here. He knows what Dad thinks about animals on hotel premises. Dad won't even let us have a dog or a cat, never mind anything dangerous."

"That," I pointed out, "is exactly why Henry's keeping it so secret. Well? Are you coming or not?"

Everything was going smoothly. Mam and I helped Lisa serve dinner for sixteen residents in record time. We were just rearranging the tables when the phone rang in Reception.

"Mum!" Jake called. "David needs you to pick him up from Matthew's house."

"Oh no! Can't your dad go? The Bowling Club will be arriving any minute."

"I don't know where Dad is," said Jake. "I can't find

him anywhere."

"Typical," said Lisa angrily. "Absolutely typical. Never there when you need him."

Mam said, "Don't you worry, Katie and me can sort this lot out." She almost pushed Lisa out of the door. Just in time – the first guests arrived five minutes later, while Jake was still fixing the banner in place.

Soon they were flooding in. Jake's dad miraculously reappeared to welcome them; Mam and I took trays of drinks round. Henry staggered in from the kitchen with huge trays full of food, which the guests eyed longingly. But of course the party couldn't really start until Lisa arrived.

"She's here!" called Jake from the window, and everyone suddenly fell silent.

We could hear her out in the hall, telling David to hurry upstairs and get started on his homework. She sounded cross. "And if that father of yours is up there, tell him to get down here RIGHT NOW!"

Terry pretended to tremble with fear. Obviously she still hadn't forgiven him for not remembering her birthday.

Lisa came bustling into the room – and stopped dead. "Surprise!" everyone shouted.

Her mouth dropped wide open. She stared at the banner, the pile of presents, the crowd of friends and relatives singing "Happy Birthday".

"She never guessed," said Jake triumphantly. "She never suspected a thing. Oh no – she's not going to cry, is she?"

For a minute it looked as if she might. "Oh, Terry!" she said. "It's lovely. And I thought you'd forgotten…"

"Happy birthday, darling," he said, and kissed her.

Suddenly she said, "Is this what it was all about? The phone calls, the secrets – I should have known. You dirty rat! I'll get you for this." But she was smiling.

I saw that Jake was wrong. It wasn't true that Lisa had suspected nothing; she had suspected Terry, just as we did. Could any party – even the greatest party of the century – make up for all the worry he must have caused her? (Because this is what happens with fibs. Even the so-called harmless ones can have the power to hurt.)

But never mind. It was all right now; she was happy.

"Break out the champagne!" someone shouted. "Quick, before Lisa gets too old to enjoy it."

"Lisa, I'm deeply shocked. You've been telling us for years that you're only 29."

"Downhill all the way from now on, love!"

The party got noisier and livelier. Terry turned the music up quite loud, and Jake looked shocked. "He never lets us play it this loud. He always says the residents won't like it."

"The louder the better," I said. "No one will hear you scream when the crocodile gets you. Come on – let's go."

I had nicked Mam's keys from the pocket of her overalls, but it took me several tries to find the right one for the office. Luckily there was no one to see me fumbling about. At last we were in; Jake closed the door, and the party noise died down a bit.

We looked in the desk drawer for the main set of keys, but it wasn't there.

"Try the other drawers," I said. Two were locked;

the rest held nothing useful. I searched throughout the muddle of papers on the desk. No keys... I didn't know whether to be relieved or disappointed.

Suddenly Jake said, "I know! The safe! If only he hasn't changed the combination..."

He fiddled with the dials of the big grey safe in the corner. His first try didn't work. "It used to be Dad's date of birth. Maybe he changed it to Mum's," Jake muttered.

Somebody rang the Reception bell. "Go on then, answer it," said Jake.

It was only an elderly guest asking for her room key. I found it on the hooks behind the reception desk. The lady looked rather deafened by the noise.

"Is that going to go on all night?" she asked. "This always used to be such a nice, peaceful hotel. No wild parties. No what-do-you-call-them? Rave-ups?"

"Oh, it's not a *very* wild party," I assured her. (Keep the customers happy, Jake always says.) "I'm sure they'll turn the noise down before it gets late."

The old lady sniffed disapprovingly. "This is not, absolutely *not*, what I came on holiday for. I shall complain to the manager."

"Feel free," I wanted to say. "You'll find him in there." But it would only spoil the party, and that was the last thing I wanted to do. I told her the manager would be available in the morning.

When at last she went away, I slid back into the office. Closing the door, I heard a slight jangling noise, like keys clashing together... I lifted the jacket that hung on a hook behind the door, and beneath it I found the key-ring.

Jake was still fighting with the controls of the safe. I shook the keys under his nose.

"We're in business," I told him.

# Chapter 20

## Unlocked

Again, it took me many attempts to find the right key. My hands were shaking slightly. If Henry happened to want something from his flat…

But no one came by. We were in the basement, where hotel guests seldom came, except to visit the games room. The corridor was deserted and quiet; somewhere up above, the sound of the party pulsed like a heartbeat. And then I heard another sound – the click of a lock.

The door swung open silently. Inside was darkness, apart from a small glow of light in a far corner.

"After you," said Jake.

"No, after *you*."

Jake fumbled around for a light switch. When he found it, we both stepped cautiously into the flat. I don't know what I expected to see – someplace like the Reptile House, perhaps. But I was in for a disappointment.

It was just a room, an ordinary room. There was a telly, two armchairs, cupboards, a bookcase, a table. Most of the furniture was dark, and the curtains, already drawn, were dark brown too. It was all a bit depressing.

"Where's the crocodile, then?" whispered Jake.

"I don't know." I began to feel like an idiot. Once again I'd managed to exaggerate, to make something out of nothing...

There were two doors on the far side of the room. Jake opened one, to show a small, windowless bathroom. I tried the other one. I found a bedroom containing a bed and wardrobe, nothing else. Surely Henry wouldn't keep snakes in his wardrobe?

Suddenly Jake said, "What's this?"

He was looking at something in a corner of the living-room. At first I thought it was a glass-fronted cupboard, the sort of thing people keep ornaments in. There was a light inside it, so that you could see quite plainly what was in there. Which was... not a lot. The floor was covered in small pieces of bark, with a couple of branches sticking up. But there was nothing *alive* in there.

"Looks like you were on the right track after all," said Jake. "Maybe he used to have a snake or something, but it died."

"Or else he's planning to get one soon," I said.

Jake unfastened a metal catch and opened the glass front of the cabinet. He put his hand in. "Feels warm," he said. "There must be some kind of heater..."

"Jake! Look – it's moving!"

He jerked backwards. He had seen it too – a slight movement of the bark fragments that covered the floor. And then a head appeared. A narrow head with a wicked, red, forked tongue.

"A snake!" he screamed. We both leaped away from the open door of the cabinet – which was stupid. Of course we should have tried to close it. I can see that now, but at the time –

The snake slithered out from its hiding place,

showing more and more of its smooth body, chequered in shades of grey and black. It was looking at us. That bright red tongue flickered in and out like a flame.

I took two steps back, bumped into a chair and almost fell. Jake stood his ground – but now the snake was moving towards the door of the cabinet. It began to glide over the edge, pouring itself down onto the carpet, smooth as a river.

It was out. It was free.

"Stand still," Jake whispered. "Don't scare it."

*Me* scare it? I was more terrified than I'd ever been in my life. Was it poisonous… would it bite?

The snake looked this way and that with its round black eyes. It was longer than my arm. Its tail twitched nervously, its tongue tasted the air.

"Maybe I can catch it," Jake breathed.

"Don't be stupid. You'll get bitten. Don't touch it… oh!"

In one swift, flowing movement, the snake slid across the floor, away from us. The bathroom door was slightly open, showing only darkness. The snake made towards it, slipped through the slit of the door, and disappeared.

Jake tiptoed after it. Ever so cautiously he closed the bathroom door. "Gotcha!" he said triumphantly.

I sat down suddenly, feeling as weak as a used bit of Blu-tak. "Are you sure it can't get out again?" I whispered.

"Pretty sure. That door is a good tight fit. And there weren't any windows… at least I don't think there were."

"W-what are we going to do now?"

Jake said, "Get out of here, a.s.a.p. Come on!"

I went to close the door of the snake's container, but Jake said, "Leave it. Maybe Henry will think the catch was loose, or something."

"You mean we're not going to tell him what happened?"

"Of *course* we're not going to tell him. Are you crazy?"

"But Jake! What if he doesn't notice it's got out? He'll go in the bathroom and step on it, or something. Then it'll bite him and he'll die…"

"Oh." He stopped to think. "You're right. We'd better leave a note or something. Quick!"

I ran to get some paper and a pencil from the games room, which luckily was empty. I scrawled in big letters, WARNING. SNAKE LOOSE IN BATHROOM, and propped the message against the bathroom door. The writing was so shaky, it looked as if a five-year-old had done it.

"With any luck he'll think it was David," Jake muttered. "Let's get out of here."

With hands that trembled much worse than before, I locked Henry's door. "We'd better put the keys back in the office," said Jake. "And wipe them with a tissue or something. Get rid of fingerprints."

"That's stupid. Your fingerprints are all over the snake's cage," I reminded him. "You want to go back in and wipe them off?"

"No way," he shuddered.

"Anyway, Henry's not going to check for fingerprints. How could he? Hey, you don't think he'll get the police in, do you?"

"I don't know. He'll be flaming mad, I do know that. And you've seen what he's like when he gets angry."

Yes, I had seen him. He had a terrible temper; he had been known to throw things around the kitchen. When that happened, even Terry kept well out of his way.

We talked in whispers in the quiet corridor.

"I still think we ought to tell him," I said, although the thought of his fury made me feel sick inside.

"Well I don't. You tell him if you want to – but don't involve me. This whole thing was all your fault, anyway."

"No it wasn't! Who let the snake out?" I said indignantly.

"I would never have gone in there if it wasn't for you and your stupid stories."

"It wasn't a stupid story. It was true."

"Yeah. And I wish it wasn't. I should never have listened to you."

I stared at him. "You're frightened, aren't you? And I always thought you were so brave." How could he have the courage to face up to a snake, and yet be too cowardly to tell the truth?

Jake looked uncomfortable. "You're right, I'm scared. If you've got any sense, you'll be scared too. It's not only Henry – it's Dad. He'll be furious if he finds out about this."

"Your dad? Why?"

"Oh, you know what he's like. Bad publicity for the hotel… he hates that."

I swallowed hard. "Then what do you think we should do?"

"Nothing. Pretend we don't know anything at all. Snake, what snake? Put the keys in the office and go back to the party."

So that was what we did.

# Chapter 21

## Snake charmer

By now it was quite a party. Lisa was having a great time. At some stage she had managed to change out of her working clothes. Now she wore a bright red dress, and huge earrings that sparkled as she laughed.

Even Mam seemed to be enjoying herself, moving through the crowd, refilling glasses. Henry brought in bowls of trifle, fruit salad, and an ice sculpture shaped like a swan, which made everyone gasp in amazement. Henry looked happy. He wouldn't be smiling like that if he knew…

"Katie, are you okay?" asked David.

"Of course I am," I snapped. "Why shouldn't I be?"

"You seem a bit…" He didn't finish the sentence. "Have some trifle."

"No thanks." I just didn't feel like eating. I was already full right up with guilt and fear.

I told myself that it could be worse. At least I hadn't had to tell any lies. If I just kept quiet, maybe nothing would happen. After all, Henry wouldn't want people to know about his pet. Perhaps he would quietly recapture it, put it in its box, and say nothing at all.

Somehow this idea didn't make things seem any

better. What we had done was still wrong – perhaps even illegal. Breaking and entering? Putting a life at risk? Theft of a valuable creature?

I felt weighed down. I felt as if I was carrying a huge back-pack full of wet sand. David was watching me again; he seemed about to say something. To avoid him, I picked up a tray, collected some empty glasses and headed for the kitchen.

As I crossed the hall I had to pass the door of the ladies' toilet. Suddenly there was a piercing scream. A woman rushed out, almost crashing into me and my tray.

"A snake! A snake!" she screeched.

What? Surely not another one?

"Where is it?" I said.

"In there. In the cupboard under the sink," she jabbered. "I was just looking for some soap... It moved, it's alive!"

She ran into the lounge, yelling even louder than the music. "Help! Help! A snake in the toilets!"

I put my tray down very carefully, because the glasses were rattling together. Was it possible that Henry's snake had found its way up here?

Sea View was an old building. The inner walls were hollow, with pipes and cables hidden inside them. When the plumbers had put new pipes in, they left a few holes in the plaster, which Terry was to fix "as and when I get the time".

So, a hole in the plaster... a nice warm water pipe to coil around, hidden in the wall or the floor... a dark cupboard under the sink... The snake might have felt quite safe there, until that woman opened the door and screamed.

Oh no. This was getting worse and worse.

A crowd of people, mostly men, came out of the lounge. Henry was at the head of them. Even Henry hesitated, though, outside the door of the Ladies.

"We should call a vet," said someone.

"Or the RSPCA."

Henry seemed to make up his mind. "I'll try to catch it," he said. "If it's what I think it is, then it's completely harmless."

"How do you know?"

"Oh, I know a bit about snakes. I... er... used to keep them as pets." He clicked his fingers at me. "Katie! Get me some whitebait out of the fridge. Plastic box marked DO NOT TOUCH, behind the cheese."

I fetched it in five seconds flat.

"You and you," Henry said to two men, "guard the door. Don't let anyone in – I need absolute peace and quiet. And tell them to turn that music down!"

He went into the Ladies and closed the door.

"What on earth's going on?" said Terry. About six people told him; his face went quite pale. He was thinking of the newspaper headlines – SNAKE ON THE LOOSE IN SEASIDE HOTEL.

The party had come to a sudden stop. Half the guests were out in the hallway, waiting to see what would happen. (What were they expecting? A yell of pain from Henry? A snake slithering out from under the door, licking its lips?)

We waited and waited. I tried to imagine what was happening in there. Perhaps the snake was still in the cupboard, and Henry was trying to lure it out with food. Perhaps it had gone back inside the wall – in which case it might appear anywhere. The kitchen, my bedroom… oh, no. Please, no.

After what felt like a century, Terry knocked softly on the door. "Henry? Are you all right in there?"

No reply. Was Henry lying unconscious on the floor?

Then, suddenly, the door opened. Henry came out, carrying the snake. It had wrapped itself around his arm, with its head and neck sticking straight out, like a ruler.

A gasp went up. People stepped hurriedly backwards.

"Don't worry," said Henry. "She's a garter snake. Non-poisonous. I'm going to put her back safely – excuse me, please."

He didn't have to ask twice. The crowd melted away in front of him as he headed for the stairs.

"Henry!" said Terry in a sharp voice. "Do I understand you right? Is that creature yours?"

"Er… yes, she is," said Henry. "I can't think how she got out. It's never happened before."

"I want a word with you later," Terry said. "We can't have this kind of thing going on."

"I know," said Henry, looking upset. He went down into the basement.

"Oh-oh," Jake said to me very quietly. "He's going to find that note. He's going to know the snake didn't get out all by itself."

"What are we going to do?"

"What I said. Just deny everything. He can't possibly prove who did it."

People began to drift back into the lounge, talking excitedly.

"Terry, you didn't tell us there would be live entertainment. Snake-charming, no less!"

"What's coming next? A magician? The Indian rope trick?"

What came next was Henry. He came charging into the room, as wild as a raging bull. My note about the snake was clutched in his enormous fist.

"Who did it?" he shouted. "Who let Gertie out? One of you kids has been in my room. Who was it?"

"Henry!" Lisa stepped in front of him like a matador in front of a bull. Amazingly, he didn't knock her over but came to a halt, glowering.

"Look at this," he cried, waving the bit of paper. "Somebody's been in my room, opened Gertie's box and let her out. I knew she couldn't escape on her own. Who did it?"

"That does look like a child's writing," said Lisa, looking at the note. Her voice turned hard. "Jake. David. Did you do this?"

"Not me," said Jake instantly.

"Me neither," said David.

"It must have been her, then – Katie. Where is she?" Henry bellowed.

I was hiding behind a group of people, but suddenly it felt as if I was all alone. What was I going to do? Own up, or lie about it?

Oh God, please help me. I want to do the right thing, I really do. But I'm frightened...

Henry had spotted me. "There she is! Come here, you. You've been nothing but trouble since the day you got here." His voice went dangerously quiet. "Now tell me, yes or no. Have you been in my room?"

Everyone was staring at me. I looked round and

could see no help anywhere, from anyone. Terry and Lisa, whose party I had wrecked – Mam, who would be furious with me – Jake, who wouldn't even look at me –

Tell a lie. Tell a lie. It's so easy, and it will get you out of trouble.

"Yes or no?" Henry thundered, looming above me like an enormous dark cloud.

Just then I remembered Grace's mum. I could almost hear her voice. *Give Katie truth instead of lies, courage instead of fear…* And all at once I knew what I had to do.

"Yes," I whispered. "I'm sorry… I never meant this to happen. I'm really, really sorry."

Henry let out a roar. I think he wanted to hit me, but Lisa grabbed him by the arm.

"Leave it for now, Henry," she said. "We'll talk about it in the morning."

They were all still staring at me; none of them looked friendly. All my courage suddenly drained out of me. I turned and ran from the room.

Racing up the stairs to our bedroom, I could hear someone following me. It was Mam. She was so angry she could hardly speak. She locked the door, then got her suitcase out from under the bed and started throwing clothes into it.

"Mam! What are you doing?"

"First thing in the morning, we're out of here," she said grimly. "I'm not giving that Henry the satisfaction of seeing me get sacked."

"No. No! I don't want to leave, Mam!"

She glared at me. "Then you should have behaved yourself. I warned you, didn't I? Why didn't you listen?"

"But *Mam*! We belong here now, we've got friends. Don't you like it here?"

"Yes. And they've been good to us. But then you go and repay them by letting a snake loose!" She snatched things out of drawers and crammed them into the case. "How can I show my face around here, after that? Now just shut up. Get to bed, because we'll be up early. I want to be out before anybody sees us."

I buried my face in the pillow. It was so unfair. I had tried to do what was right, and now look what had happened.

Jake had let me down; I thought he was so brave, but he was a coward underneath. He'd let me take all the blame, when he was the one who had let the snake out.

Even worse, God had let me down. I had obeyed him and yet I was being punished... Everything, everyone let you down in the end.

# Chapter 22

## Leaving

It was half past five in the morning. We crept downstairs through the silent corridors, carrying our cases. Mam had only packed what we could carry. She had made me leave a lot of things behind – my school uniform, my books, a fluffy rabbit that Grace had given me.

I was used to doing this; I'd done it lots of times. But never before had I felt so sorry to be leaving.

In my mind I said goodbye to the place that had become my home. Goodbye to our little attic bedroom with its view of the lighthouse. Goodbye to the games room and the dining-room and the lift that kept breaking down. Goodbye to Jake and David, Terry and Lisa; I knew I would never see any of them again.

Out in the cold grey daylight, I said farewell to Fountain Square. They would miss me this morning at the café. I wished there had been time to say goodbye, a proper goodbye, to Grace. She could keep the china flower girl to remember me by.

I turned for one last look at Sea View. The hotel was still asleep, with curtains drawn, except… was that a face high up at an attic window?

"Come on, girl," said Mam impatiently. "Don't stand there dreaming."

"Where are we going?" I asked.

"The station. And then we'll do what we did before – stick a pin in the map, and buy a ticket."

"I wish we could stay in Westhaven," I said longingly. "You could get a job in a different hotel..."

"Who'd have us?" she said. Her voice was bitter. "Word gets around in a town like this. No, we'll go somewhere new – make a fresh start."

So it was goodbye to Westhaven. I would never see my school again, or act in the play. Never walk out on the pier or down by the harbour. Never visit Seal Island... goodbye to all that. I felt a tear slide down my face.

When Mam noticed, her voice softened just a little. "Never mind," she said. "It's been nice here, but there are other nice places."

"They won't be the same," I said.

We walked on through the deserted streets. There was no traffic moving; the only sound was the cry of seagulls on the wind. Then I heard a car speeding down the hill. It screeched to a halt beside us, and Lisa got out.

I stared at her. She seemed to be wearing a coat over pyjamas, and she had no make-up on. I had never seen Lisa without her make-up on.

She stood in front of us, so that Mam had to stop.

"You're not going," she said. "I won't let you."

Mam said, "I suppose you want me to work out my month's notice. Sorry, but I just can't face it – not having Henry gloat over me for a whole month. He'll be glad I got sacked."

"Sacked? Who said anything about sacked?" said Lisa, surprised. "If you ask me, Henry's the one who should be sacked, only we can't do without him. And we can't do without you, either. You're the best chambermaid we've had in years."

In spite of herself, Mam looked pleased. "But after last night –" she said.

Lisa said, "Listen. You know who was really to blame for last night? Not Katie, no. It was Jake. He was the one who let the snake out. And he didn't even have the guts to own up, the little rat."

"How did you find out?" I asked.

"David told me. He heard you and Jake arguing outside Henry's flat last night. But he never said a word – so as not to upset Jake, I suppose. Then, this morning, he happened to wake up and see you making off, and he came to tell me. So here we are." She looked down at her pyjama bottoms and slippers. "As you can see, I didn't waste any time."

"So you really want us to stay?" I asked, feeling rather dazed.

"Of course we do."

"What about Henry?" said Mam. "He won't like it."

"Henry will do as I say," said Lisa. "I think I'll offer him a bargain. If he wants to keep his beloved Gertie, he's got to promise to treat you right. Okay? Otherwise Gertie can go to the Reptile House."

Mam nodded slowly. I felt a great big grin spreading over my face.

"Hop in the car, then," said Lisa, "and we'll all go home."


"Thanks," I said to David.

"What for?"

"For telling your mum. If it wasn't for you, we would be miles away by now, in some horrible place where we don't know anybody."

"I ought to have told her sooner," he said. "Only I was scared of Jake. I'm not as brave as you, Katie."

"Me, brave? I'm not brave," I said, remembering the way my hands shook and my legs felt like melting jelly.

"Yes you are. When you told the truth to Henry – that was about the bravest thing I've ever seen." He gave me an admiring look, the kind of look I used to give to Jake. I felt a warm glow inside; it was so nice to be admired. But then I remembered.

"It wasn't *me* being brave," I said. "Somebody was helping me… But tell me, how did you happen to wake up just in time to see us leaving?"

"I don't know." He looked puzzled. "Normally I never wake up in the night. Mum has to drag me out of bed on school days. But this morning something woke me – I don't know what. And I looked out of the window, and there you were, just about to disappear around the corner."

"A few seconds later, you'd have missed us," I said.

"Yeah. Lucky, wasn't it?"

But secretly I knew that luck was nothing to do with it.

# Chapter 23

## Present

In a week when news was thin on the ground, the snake episode made the front page of the local paper. SNAKE-CHARMER CHEF, the headline said, above a big photo of Henry with Gertie coiled around his hand. (Of the two, I thought Gertie was by far the better-looking.)

"At the Sea View Hotel, Gertie the garter snake gate-crashed a party…" the report began.

Oh-oh, I thought. Terry won't like this.

But Terry needn't have worried. For days after, the phone kept ringing – not with cancellations but with bookings for meals. Everyone wanted to see the famous snake. Because people kept asking, Henry moved Gertie's box upstairs, with a large padlock and chain around it, just in case. But Gertie spent most of her time hidden away under the bits of bark on her floor. "Are you sure she hasn't got out again?" customers would ask, half-anxious, half-hopeful.

Henry was in quite a good mood these days; perhaps he enjoyed all the attention. He had almost stopped making nasty comments about Mam and me. When Lisa found out it was Mam's birthday, she even persuaded Henry to bake a cake.

The moment came: I gave Mam her birthday present.

"Oh! Katie," she breathed. "Thank you. It's the nicest thing you could ever give me. How on earth did you get the money?"

"Helping Lisa," I said. But that was not the whole truth; I felt bad about it. In the end I told Mam everything.

"But the flower girl wasn't stolen," I said hastily. "Mrs Parkes bought it, I saw her."

"That's not what worries me," said Mam. Her face was grave. "You shouldn't have done that, Katie – gone off with a stranger like that."

"Yes. I know," I said in a small voice. "I'll never do it again."

There was one thing left to do – ring Desmond and Daisy. The thought of it lay on my conscience for days, but I was frightened. What would they say when they knew the truth about me? Would they tell the police?

At last I gathered enough courage to do it. Hearing the phone ring, I prayed no one would answer it…

"Hello?" It was Daisy.

"It's me – Katie," I blurted out. "I mean, I told you my name was Megan but that wasn't true. Remember me?"

"Of course, dear," she said. "I believe we still have a jumper of yours."

She didn't sound angry with me, so I took a deep breath and told her about my first visit to the old man's house. Even then she wasn't angry – at least not with me.

"Oh, that woman," she said. "Dreadful! Getting children to do her dirty work for her."

"I didn't help her steal from the old man," I said. "I really didn't – not after I saw what she was up to. Will I get in trouble?"

"No, dear. It wasn't your fault. Horrible woman! Did you know, she's asking for nine other offences to be taken into consideration. Nine!"

"Er... what does that mean?" I asked.

"It means she cheated nine other people as well as poor Frank. The police found the evidence in her shop. What she did was, most of the time she bought things quite legally. But every now and then she would come across people who were... well, a little confused. Elderly people who didn't know the value of what they owned, or who'd forgotten how much a five-pound note was worth. And then she would rob them blind."

"What will happen to her? Will she go to prison?" I asked.

"Sure to, dear."

"And the old man – is he okay?"

She sighed. "In a manner of speaking. The police found his picture that she stole, but I don't think he'd even missed it. He keeps asking when he's going to see Joan and Alice again, and what can you say?"

The school play went really well. Everyone remembered their lines, and the audience only laughed when they were meant to (well, most of the time). Even Megan got everything right.

"I shouldn't have been so rude about Megan acting a snake," I said to Grace. "Snakes are quite nice, actually. Or some of them are." (Once or twice Henry had let me handle Gertie and admire her beautiful markings.)

Grace said, "Megan's not too bad, either. Is she?"

"No," I admitted. "She's changed quite a bit."

"She's not the only one."

"Are you telling me I've changed? What do you mean?"

"Well, sometimes you were a bit…" She hesitated.

"A bit what?"

I could see her struggling to find words that would be truthful and yet not hurtful. "A bit of a show-off, sometimes. You were trying to get people to like you, but it didn't always work. They like you much better now."

"Because I've stopped telling lies?"

She shook her head. "Because you've stopped trying to make them like you. You've stopped wanting to have everyone's attention all the time."

"Oh." Had I really been as bad as that?

"And you've stopped going on about your father."

"You're right," I said, surprised. I used to think about him all the time, but recently he had hardly even crossed my mind. Why? Because I'd begun to know a different Father – one who would never go away and leave me. One who loved me. One I could always rely on.

I looked out of the window. It was a beautiful, starry night. The moon was full; its bright reflection lay like a silver path across the bay. But moon, and stars, and the lights of the town, were not what I was looking for. You had to know just where to look…

And there it was: the distant flash of light. It never failed – you could rely on it. Again and again it shone out, the beam of light that gave warning to ships at sea, and comforted people in the darkness. Again and again, all through the night, until the morning.